Sep 6

11/28

D1004361

FIGHTING GUNMAN

Whenever there was trouble, Jack Sharp and his best friend, Mert Scanlon, were always in the midst of it. Mert threatened to shoot off one of the storeowner's ears because Colly Johnson had bought all the rifle ammunition. Worse still, Colly made a play for Mert's girlfriend and in the ensuing fight Johnson and another man were killed. Mert fled with the sheriff's posse on his trail. Even then, Jack helped his partner. But, soon, Jack's famed gun skills would be needed to fight the notorious Gomez boys . . .

*Books by William Shand
in the Linford Western Library:*

THE CROOKED MARSHAL

WILLIAM SHAND

FIGHTING GUNMAN

Complete and Unabridged

LINFORD
Leicester

First hardcover edition published in Great Britain
in 2003 by Robert Hale Limited, London

Originally published in paperback as
Fighting Gunman by V. Joseph Hanson

First Linford Edition
published 2004
by arrangement with
Robert Hale Limited, London

The moral right of the author has been asserted

British Library CIP Data

Shand, William, *1920–2001*
    Fighting gunman.—Large print ed.—
Linford western library
1. Western stories
2. Large type books
I. Title II. Hanson, Vic J.
823.9'14 [F]
ISBN 1–84395–582–2

Published by
F. A. Thorpe (Publishing)
Anstey, Leicestershire

Set by Words & Graphics Ltd.
Anstey, Leicestershire
Printed and bound in Great Britain by
T. J. International Ltd., Padstow, Cornwall

This book is printed on acid-free paper

1

'Hold Yuh Hosses, Mert'

The interior of the store was clean and cool after the sun-glare outside. The two rannies swept off their sombreros and shook the dust from them. They wiped their streaming faces with the fringes of their bandannas that looped their throats.

Joe Sams looked up from his account book.

'Hi-yuh, Mert — Jack,' he said.

'Hi-yuh,' the two men strode to the counter and leaned on it.

'Carry on with your figurin', Joe. We got plenty time — an' it's kinda peaceful in here.' Their faces were illumined by the sun that streamed through the side window. The one who spoke was of medium height and build. His homely features were freckle-dusted

1

and good natured, his hair sandy, but he looked like he would be a handy man in a pinch. His companion was taller, a magnificent specimen with very handsome aquiline features and long raven-black hair. His mobile lips were smiling now. His dark eyes glowed with humour above high cheek bones. Maybe somewhere way back one of his ancestors had been Indian.

'I won't be but a minute, gents,' said Joe Sams. 'Make yourselves at home.'

The two men wandered over to a dark corner and sat theirselves on some piled sacks of meal. The freckled man produced the makings and began to roll a cigarette expertly with his right hand. With his left he handed the little sack of baccy and papers to his companion.

'Thanks, Jack,' said the other.

They sat and smoked in silence, enjoying the coolness and the rest from sitting on a hard saddle bumping over rough trails. Then Joe Sams closed his book with a slam.

'Thanks fer waitin', gents,' he said.

'I'm at your service.'

The two rannies shot from their perch. The freckled Jack said: 'We jest want some provisions for the Ol' Man an' a few things for ourselves.' He tossed a paper on the counter. 'Thet's the Ol' Man's list.'

'All right,' said the storekeeper. He began to pile the groceries on the counter, ticking each item on the paper with a stub of pencil. Then he said: 'I'm sorry, gents, I've got no rifle slugs a'tall — an' very little forty-five stuff . . . '

'Me an' Mert wanted some ammunition as well,' said Jack.

'Sorry, gents, it cain't be done . . . '

'Whadyuh mean — cain't be done?' said the tall dark Mert. 'What's all them new boxes at the back there? It looks mighty like your usual rifle-stuff tuh me.'

'Wal, I'm mighty sorry — but I'm afraid that's ordered.'

'Whadyuh mean — ordered? It's still there ain't it.'

Joe Sams nervously re-arranged the

3

packages on the counter. He said:

'Mr Colly Johnson has ordered my full consignment this time.'

'I don't get this, Joe,' said the freckled Jack. 'It ain't right. Ain't we allus had our ammunition from you . . . ?'

Mert broke in, and there was a sneer in his deep voice. 'What's Mister Colly Johnson want with all that ammunition?'

'Wal, he does a lot of huntin' . . . '

'*Huntin*'. What's he got tuh hunt in this territory? Two-legged rats an' rabbits maybe — an he ain't gotta go far from his own spread tuh find 'em . . . '

'Take it easy, Mert,' said Jack.

Mert ignored him. His dark eyes blazed as he looked at the storekeeper.

'Every fortnight we come for this stuff off'n you. The same stuff nearly every time. A standin' order yuh might say. An' we're damsight older customers than Colly Johnson.'

'I'm sorry, Mert, Mr Johnson ordered that a week ago. Long before it arrived.

It's gotta be delivered at the Double W this afternoon. I kin let yuh have a bit of forty-five stuff . . . '

'You can let us have a few boxes o' that rifle-stuff too,' said Mert levelly. His handsome face was taut, and seemed even darker. 'I ain't gonna stand by an' see Johnson hog everythin' — even if pipsqueaks like you do kow-tow to his money.'

'Air yuh trying tuh tell me how to run my own business?' said Joe Sams with a sudden flash of spirit. Then his mouth dropped open, his eyes bulged, as he looked into the mouth of Mert's Colt.

'F'r Pete's sake,' said Jack. 'Hold yuh hosses, Mert.'

Again the dark ranny ignored him. His voice was trembling with passion as he said to the storekeeper. 'Put half-a-dozen o' them boxes in here with the other stuff . . . Quick! 'fore I blow one o'your ears off. An' you can tell Mister Colly Johnson who's had 'em.'

Joe Sams watched the tall man as if

5

he was a fizzling stick of dynamite as he backed to the shelves and got the boxes down.

'Start takin' the stuff out, Jack,' said Mert.

The freckle-faced one shrugged. 'All right,' he said. 'But I ain't singing no songs about it.'

A few minutes later the two men left the store. Now he had got his own way Mert had regained his good humour. His parting shot was:

'We'll take our custom elsewhere in future. An' I hope Mister Colly Johnson goes back East an' leaves yuh flat.'

Joe Sams was too downright peeved to find words to answer him.

The two rannies had a quick couple of beers at the nearby Golden Pesos saloon and then hit the trail for home. Their stomachs rumbled and they wanted to be back in time for midday chow.

In the crowded purlieus of the honky-tonk neither man had referred to the stores incident. And right then there were no repercussions so Joe Sams had evidently not told the law — yet.

Now, on the trail, Jack said: 'That temper o' yourn is gonna land yuh in a peck o' trouble someday, ol' timer.'

'If that's the beginning of a lecture yuh kin quit it,' said Mert amiably.

'Nope, jest a passing thought. How you keep out o' the hoosegow beats me. Mebbe becos most folks know yuh an' figure you're misunderstood — just a happy harmless cowhand at heart.'

'Air you tryin' tuh be funny, little man?'

'Nope. But I don't figure there wuz any need f'r that play back there. We could've got our shells some place else.'

'I ain't aiming to bow down while that panty-waisted swine, Johnson, tries to hog everything around here.'

'That's the way they do things back East in the big cities. He's new here — he'll learn. Anyway, I don't see that 'cos you've got a grudge against Johnson you should pull a gun on ol' Joe. Purty strong measure under the circumstances — threatenin' tuh shoot his ear off, too.'

'The Ol' Man's one o' Joe's oldest customers. He deserves his damned head shootin' off f'r ratting on him like that.' There was an edge on Mert's voice now. 'An' I ain't got a grudge against Johnson. I jest don't like the way he's flashing his money around, tryin' tuh impress everybody an' tryin' tuh buy everythin'.'

Jack gave his philosophic shrug again. 'Fergit it,' he said.

He knew what was really eating Mert. Pride — and woman-trouble! And when a man of his calibre had a good dose of that particularly explosive mixture it was best for everybody, even his best friend, to let him be. But the good natured freckled ranny was worried. That temper of Mert's was almost murderous at times.

Trouble about Mert Scanlon was that he was too handsome and charming and some folks had made too much of him. Even the steady forthrightness of his comrade, Jack Sharp, was not enough foil for him at times. Jack could be a hellion too, but his wildness was more disciplined. He was not easily roused, but a bad man to meddle with and probably the only gun in the territory that was faster than Mert Scanlon. They were a good team but, at times, only the quick thinking of Jack kept them that way.

A man passed them on the trail and waved a hand in greeting. Jack waved back, but Mert merely scowled. Brad Ruston was the Double W straw-boss and everything or anybody connected with the Johnson spread was just plain pizen to the tall ranny.

Nevertheless, even Mert could not help but admit that Johnson had a prize in the lean, prematurely-greying cattle-man; the dude would be lost without him, for pampered son of a millionaire Chicago meat-packer that he was, though an athlete and a crack horse-man, he did not know the first thing about ranching. Still, he had enough money to buy all the help he needed and all the accessories and appliances for smoothing away the hardships that less fortunate settlers could not afford.

The two rannies urged their horses off the trail and headed them across the rolling mesa of the Rio Grande. To their right at one point the sun gleamed on thin, silver strands of wire: the boundary between the Double W and their home-spread, the Horse V. This fence was another of Colly Johnson's Eastern ideas. That the steers belonging to both ranches were in the habit of forcibly scratching their hides against the fence-posts and affording regular bouts of cussing and hard labour to Johnson's repair-gang, was a huge source of amusement to Hank Bulger, owner of the Horse V. Hank, being the settler of longest standing in the district, was known to everybody as the Old Man. For years he had lived at peace with his neighbours without seeing any need for fences, so he was somewhat peeved by the Johnson innovation. However, after a little thought on the subject, he had given one of those little definite nods of his white head and remarked that it 'didn't amount to no more than a prairie-puffball anyway.'

On the other side of the Horse V spread was Nat Hodgeson's Pinwheel. There were no fences here and cattle bearing the brand of the horseshoe and the V often mingled with those bearing the intricate wheelmark. Right at the back, on the long narrow strip that bordered the fabulous Rio, was Don 'George' Gabazo's ranch and hacienda.

All three old ranchmen had been negotiating for the rest of the territory. It was a race between them as, in turn, they nibbled little pieces off. Then, like a bolt from the blue, came Colly Johnson and with his money and influence snapped up the rest — and a mighty lush hunk of territory it was too. The old-timers, except perhaps the arrogant Mexican don, did not seem to hold it against him. But they did not profess to like his new-fangled

Eastern ideas; and his hog-like Eastern nature.

* * *

That night was the occasion of the annual Summer barbecue which was held in the lush, low-lying Big Meadow, midway between the Horse V and the Pinwheel and quite close to the cowtown of San Martini. San Martini was a smaller prototype of its two nearest neighbours, standing midway between them, San Antonio and Laredo. It consisted of one wide corkscrew main street with clapboard and adobe buildings along both sides. Joe Sam's one-storey wooden store was the first of these. The rest were of the same ilk — stables, honky-tonks, the sheriff's office, the small jail, the Trust Association's log office, various shops; then a jungle of sordid Mexican dwellings right at the end.

Mert and Jack made their way to the site of the barbecue. They wore their best rig-outs. Mert had a pearl-grey shirt that showed off his dark, good looks, and Jack a vivid red one. They had left their guns behind. 'No guns' was the unwritten law of the barbecue. They saw the site, a blaze of light in the valley, long before they reached it.

Long fence-posts had been hammered into the ground to make a wide circle and from the tops of these were hung hurricane lanterns. All around there were dozens of benches and tables, and on the stretch of soil beside the small creek, a roaring bonfire. The wide expanse of turf in the centre of the lantern-lit circle was empty for dancing. There was a small stage like an inverted box. When Mert and Jack arrived the orchestra, consisting of cornet, two violins, bass fiddle, concertina, banjo and drums, was already tuning-up.

A pig was being roasted on a spit over the fire and the womenfolk were laying tables ready for the feast.

Hank Bulger, the Old Man, was already there. He was a widower, and had no kin. His boys were his family. With him was his old pardner, tall lanky old Nat Hodgeson of the Pinwheel with his wife and his blonde daughter, Judy. As the boys approached, Mrs Hodgeson and Judy moved away to help at the tables.

The Old Man saw the boys and called them over.

'Glad you decided tuh honour us with your presence,' he chaffed. 'All the rest of the elite are here — Look, here comes Don George.'

A tall, swarthy old-timer with iron-grey hair sweeping from beneath his black sombrero was coming towards them. With him was a whip-like youngster, his son Pedro.

'Ah, Señor Hank, Nat — an' the boys,' said Don George, both hands held out with Latin effusiveness.

'Welcome tuh the barbecue, Don George — Pedro,' said the Old Man.

Jack Sharp noted that his pard's attention was wandering. Mert was looking over to the tables where blonde, beautiful Judy Hodgeson, the belle of the territory, was talking to a tall, well-built young man who matched her in looks and colouring. None other than Colly Johnson of the Double W. Mert's jaw-muscles were rippling. Things were a little strained between him and Judy lately — and all because of that dandified Easterner. Just now Judy had walked away at his approach. And now she was chatting away to the guy like she was his best girl, laughing and showing her even white teeth, her blue eyes sparkling in the lantern light.

'Ah,' said Don George. 'There is Señor Johnson. I must greet him.'

He left the little group and, followed by his taciturn son, went over to Johnson. The owner of the Double W turned as the old Don approached. They shook hands. Then the Mexican bowed over the hand of Judy Hodgeson.

'Allus the gentleman, Don George,' said Nat Hodgeson.

Not so his son. He was of the

younger generation, fiery, intolerant. He patiently ignored Johnson, but revealed more animation in greeting Judy than he had done since he and the old man had arrived at the barbecue.

'Let's go get a quencher,' said Jack Sharp.

Mert suffered himself to be led to the wagon that dispensed soft drinks — the other stuff would be supplied later on when the festivities really got under way.

Again Jack's quick thinking may have saved a ticklish situation, for Johnson was approaching the group the two rannies had just left.

Mert sipped his squash and answered Jack's commonplaces with curt monosyllables. Along at the tables the women began to bring pans, and carol the time-honoured 'Come an' git it!'

'Come on,' said Jack. 'We don't want tuh miss nuthin'. I feel like I could eat that porker all at one sitting.'

'You ain't got no bottom to yuh,' said Mert mechanically, and Jack knew that his pard's good humour was in some measure restored.

They sat on the end of a bench, Mert next to the Old Man; then came Nat Hodgeson, Pedro Gabazo and his father, Colly Johnson and his foreman, Brad Ruston.

The women began to serve. Judy Hodgeson said hallo to Mert as if she had only just noticed him. The handsome cowboy answered her laconically. Judy passed on. A few minutes later they heard her ripple of laughter as Colly Johnson, his blond hair gleaming in the lantern-light just as hers did, said something to her. Mert's jaw muscles rippled as he bent over his plate and pretended not to notice, and Jack wondered savagely why Judy acted the goat. She was flirting with Johnson. But Mert did not realize that. Either way he didn't like it. He needed watching plenty. Every incident like that was a goad to Mert's pride — and he didn't easily forget.

During the eating the band played

slow stuff; a bean-pole of a singer warbled border ballads. Then, while the others rested after their feastings, the band got down, and in their turn, stoked themselves up in readiness for the real efforts of the evening.

Mert and Jack sat under a gnarled cotton-wood and smoked. Judy was nowhere to be seen. Neither was Johnson. Jack Sharp pulled his hat over his eyes and pretended to doze as he dragged at his cigarette. He knew his pard's dark eyes were searching everywhere while his mind speculated. Then Judy came up from the creek with her mother in tow. Jack began to rest easy and was glad to note his pard's tenseness had left him too.

The Old Man suddenly came upon them. His face was unusually grave.

'I've got a bone tuh pick with you boys,' he said.

'Shoot,' Jack told him.

'I've just bin talkin' tuh Joe Sams.'

Both men pricked up their ears. Jack knew what was coming. Mert's face was inscrutable as old Hank divulged the fact that the storekeeper had told him all about the incident of the morning.

'He was mighty decent about it,' concluded the Old Man. 'He said he wouldn't tell Johnson — he'd jest put him off — say all his consignment hadn't turned up or something.'

'Mighty nice of him,' sneered Mert.

The Old Man's blue eyes flashed in his seamed face. 'That's what I said! Joe don't want no trouble no more than I do. That was a mighty dangerous, as well as totally uncalled for, play you made this morning, Mert . . . Don't let anything like that happen again when you're on business for me. People ain't gonna stand it all the time . . . '

'It wasn't right nohow,' retorted Mert, and added his plaint about Johnson hogging everything.

'He'll learn,' said the Old Man. 'Anyway there wasn't no need tuh pull a gun on a man who's running his business the way he wants it . . . '

'I wonder he had the craw tuh tell yuh,' said Mert. 'After all the years you've bin one of his best customers.'

'Yeah, I know,' said the Old Man. 'I told him we'll get our shells from elsewhere next time. Now yuh know what I think about it let's ferget it — An' watch that temper, Mert.'

The well-built oldtimer, his back as straight as any young man's, walked abruptly away.

'I'm sorry the Old Man found out about it,' said Mert.

'That damned storeman . . .'

'Now don't go off half-cock about Joe Sams,' Jack told him. 'Better fer him tuh tell the boss than tuh go running tuh Sheriff Blackson. You know how touchy he is — an' his trigger finger.'

'He's mighty fond o' Johnson too, so I'm told,' said Mert.

'His policy of welcomin' new arrivals to San Martini.'

Mert snorted at this. 'Money!' he said. 'An' they cluster around it like flies round a dungheap.'

His language was even more descriptive and to the point a few minutes later when they saw lean, sour-faced Sheriff Blackson for the first time that night. And he was deep in conversation with Colly Johnson.

The band struck up with that traditional warmer-up 'Turkey in the Straw', and couples began to move out on to the circle of greensward.

'Come on, Mert,' said Jack. 'Get movin'. Ain't you the best all-fired hoofer in the territory?'

'I guess I ain't feelin' like it tonight,' said the handsome waddy.

Jack figured shrewdly that this was probably due to the fact that his usual partner at such functions, Judy Hodgeson, was nowhere to be seen.

'You go an' dance,' said Mert.

'Aw,' said Jack. 'Yuh know I ain't no hoofer. I got too many feet.'

'Go on,' said Mert. He seemed quite cheerful about it.

Jack shrugged and went over to a plump, dark girl named Marie, the daughter of one of the San Martini storemen. Her effusive welcome made the freckled waddy awkward even before they got on the floor.

While he concentrated on putting his feet where they'd do least harm to his partner's, Marie prattled. She wanted to know why 'tall dark an' handsome' wasn't dancing and why he looked so glum.

'Who, Mert?' said Jack. 'I dunno. Mebbe he's got colic or sump'n.' And, cursing himself for ever venturing into this perilous sea of jogging people. 'He looks kinda lonesome. Mebbe I oughta go an' keep him company.'

'We'll both go,' said the dark girl vivaciously, and stifling Jack's protests, led the way.

A few minutes later the latter was standing alone and a disgruntled Mert was being led around by Marie. But the dark waddy was too good a dancer to shuffle around for long. Jack grinned as he saw them get into the swing of it, Marie jawing her partner's head off all the time. He was well out of that anyway.

Then Joe Sam's daughter, a mouse of a girl, came up to him. He danced with her. She was almost as bad as he and suffered in silence every time he trod on her toes.

Judy Hodgeson passed them dancing with Colly Johnson. Jack looked around for Mert Scanlon. He was still dancing with Marie and listening to her platitudes with his dark head cocked on one side.

Judy continued to dance with Johnson. Later, when Jack and Mert met for a drink, the latter watched them waltz by and his face darkened and went hard, but he made no comment right then.

Jack knew that his pard was boiling inside and he was afraid something would have to happen sooner or later.

It did. 'It's time somebody else had a dance with Judy 'cept that dude galoot,' said Mert, and he left Jack's side.

He paid no heed to his pard's usual injunction to take it easy. Jack watched him tap the Easterner on the shoulder. Johnson turned and then smiled and moved away from the girl. His manners had been learnt in Chicago society — politeness while with a lady — but Jack saw him scowl savagely as he walked away. Then, dancing along, Judy and Mert passed the freckled ranny. They both looked as if their faces had been carved from cold stone. Their lips were compressed, in case anything resembling conversation tried to escape through them. Jack shrugged. Pride was a funny thing. And those two with their good looks and their hair-trigger tempers had more than their share of it. Jack was glad that Johnson hadn't cut up rough — although it must be very evident to the ranch owner what the handsome Horse V cowhand thought about him.

There was something very much alike in the two men, despite their opposite colouring and environments.

They were both arrogant and head-strong, and Jack figured that Johnson had a hell of a temper too — but had learnt to control it better than Mert. He was a schemer, not an open-handed troubleshooter like the Texan cowboy.

Jack had himself a dance with one of the girls from town, then meandered back once more to the juice-wagon. He was beginning to carry quite a load of red-eye on his breath . . . Well, if the women didn't like it let 'em keep their distance. He was surprised to see Mert at the improvized bar once more. Though the night was passing, it was still mighty hot and Mert looked a little flustered. He had his mug buried in a couple of fingers of liquor. Johnson and Judy went by — together again. Mert looked from his glass. His dark eyes were murderous.

2

'Damn You, I'll Kill Yuh!'

In more ways than one the San Martini territory summer barbecue was open house. As the night drew on, people began to come out from the town. For one night the honky-tonk people shut up shop and joined in the festivities against which they could not compete. They had a busman's holiday as the genial Tubby la Rue, owner of the Golden Pesos Saloon, put it.

In the mêlée, Jack Sharp lost sight of his pard completely. Mert could take care of himself. Jack had another drink and quit worrying about him.

When midnight came and went, and people began to drift unsteadily home, Jack began to wonder again. He would have worried plenty had he known that Mert was following Colly Johnson and

Judy Hodgeson as they made for the former's ranch. The dark cowboy was now seething with unbridled jealousy and hurt pride. He'd find out what was going on. And, by God, that Johnson . . . Mert checked his thoughts — and his horse's strides. He didn't want them to spot him.

As he approached the Double W ranch buildings, he made a detour and came in at the back. He thought he had seen the two dismount by a corral but now they were nowhere in sight. However, a window at the side of the ranch house was ablaze with light.

Mert tethered his horse in a clump of trees, where the beast could not be spotted. Then, hugging the shadows along the log walls, he advanced to the window.

He was almost there when he heard their voices. Judy's was unusually shrill; Johnson's deep one sounded cajoling. Mert looked in. The girl was on one side of a table, Johnson the other. As Mert watched, Johnson made a quick movement and grabbed Judy's wrist.

Mert left the window, ran on to the veranda, then at full tilt through the front door. The room was at the left. He flung open the door.

Johnson turned, his eyes wide, his handsome, rather puffy face contorted by a snarl.

Mert wasted no time in words. He flung himself across the room. He heard Judy cry out, then he was locked with the ranch-owner and they crashed to the floor together.

Mert saw the other's face glaring up at him, the mouth open, and he hit it savagely. Blood gushed from Johnson's nose and his burst lips. Then his knee came up in Mert's stomach. The cowboy gasped as he was catapulted away. He heard Judy shout 'Stop it! Stop it!' He rose, crouching, as Johnson came on. The dude wanted to fight did he? He was sparring; he feinted with his left, then swung with his right as Mert swayed. Mert caught the blow on his forearm, but Johnson was ready with another left, straight and powerful, which smacked through the cowboy's guard and hit him on the point of the jaw. Mert's teeth clicked and his head went back. He staggered. Johnson's too eager follow-up blow only buffeted his shoulder, but it knocked the cowboy to his knees. Johnson swung a heavy boot. Judy cried out again. Desperately Mert flung his body to one side. The boot only grazed his side and Johnson was off-balance. Mert flung himself across the floor and crashed into the other's knees. Johnson hit the floor with a bump that seemed to shake the building.

Judy was at the door now, wide-eyed, her hand at her mouth. Both men rose simultaneously and Mert hit Johnson flush in his already battered face. The ranch owner crashed onto the table. Behind him a tall vase of flowers fell over. Johnson grabbed the vase by its neck and swung it. It smashed on Mert's left bicep, numbing his arm for a moment, then the blood began to run. Johnson followed up with both fists. One-two-three: then Mert was down. As Johnson advanced, the cowboy, dazedly kicked out with both feet. With a gasping groan Johnson doubled up, almost falling on top of his opponent, but rolled away. Mert rose up on all fours, shaking his head like a wounded beast. Long black tendrils of his hair waved in front of his face. He realized that Judy had left the room. He rose to his haunches.

Johnson was lifting himself up with the aid of a chair. He suddenly straightened, the chair coming with him. Mert threw himself sideways and the chair crashed into the window behind him, showering the floor with glass. Johnson dived and again Mert sidestepped. Johnson tried to recover but couldn't quite make it. Mert's hammer-like fist smote him in the side of the neck then, as he was falling, the cowboy's boot came up. Johnson was lucky; the boot only hit his shoulder. He rolled and crashed into an ornate china cabinet. It teetered. He scrambled clear as it fell with a hideous clatter of broken glass and china. The top of it hit Mert Scanlon across the shins, bringing him down. Mad with rage, Johnson dived at him. Threshing and kicking on the floor, they wrestled. Johnson got hold of the cowboy's throat and began to squeeze, while Mert punished him with his knees and his fists. Johnson's face resembled raw beef.

His madness left him; he began to whimper with pain, and let go. Mert hit him again, knocking him away. He was the first up this time, and waiting for the ranch-owner to rise, advanced on him, shooting blows from all angles.

Vainly Johnson tried to retaliate, to cover up; he was driven back. He was taking terrible punishment. He came up against the closed door. On the hook behind him hung a coat. Something hard bulged in its pocket. He remembered and, reaching behind him, brought forth a .38 pistol.

'You swine,' said Mert, and, head down, charged.

The gun cracked spitefully. The slug plucked at the cowboy's sleeve, then he closed with Johnson, his hand clasping the ranch-owner's wrist. Swaying and panting, they wrestled for the gun, moving to the centre of the room. There was murder in Johnson's eyes now. He was trying to bring the gun up. He was no weakling either. Straining, they crashed around the room.

The door suddenly opened and Brad Ruston stood there, gun in hand, with Judy Hodgeson behind him.

'Stop it,' said Ruston. 'Stop it.'

A deafening crash reverberated in the confined space of the room, but it was not his gun that spoke. It was the .38 the two were fighting for.

Johnson gave a gasping cry and crumpled up. The gun fell at Mert's feet. He looked down at his fallen enemy with sudden surprise on his battered face.

He turned suddenly. Something he

saw in Brad Ruston's eyes made him duck. The Colt in the foreman's hand bucked and flamed, and the slug almost parted Mert's hair as he dived for the .38. He grabbed it, rolling. He heard Judy shout. She was trying to hold Ruston's gun-arm, but the grey-haired man flung her away from him, his lips writhing away from his teeth as he fired again. But she had spoiled his aim. The slug tore a hole in the floor. Lying flat on his back, Mert squeezed the trigger of the .38.

Ruston clutched at his right shoulder and swayed. Blood ran through his fingers, but he kept a grip on the gun.

Mert rose. 'Drop it!' he snarled. 'Drop it, or damn you, I'll kill yuh!'

The Colt clattered to the floor. Ruston swayed and held on to the jamb of the door, his face yellow, his eyes widening as he saw the terrible killer-light in the dark eyes of the man who faced him. The white-faced girl gave a little shuddering cry.

★   ★   ★

As the people drifted away and the lanterns went out one by one, Jack Sharp began to search for his pard. One oldtimer said he thought he had seen him ride away.

'Towards the Horse V?' said Jack.

'Nope, it wasn't in that direction a'tall. More thataway.' The oldster pointed. 'Thataway' was in the direction of the Double W. Jack shook off the horrible suspicion that suddenly clouded his mind. He couldn't do much about it now, anyway. But why hadn't Mert told him he was going riding? Jack could not answer that question and his suspicions returned with redoubled intensity.

Then he bumped in to Mr and Mrs Hodgeson, who were looking for their daughter. They had heard she had ridden off with Colly Johnson. Old Nat was mighty peeved. 'She might've told us beforehand,' he said.

'Maybe she thought you wouldn't

approve, dear,' said Mrs Hodgeson.

'An' she'd be durn right,' said Nat. 'I don't like that smarmy Eastern galoot.'

'I think he's quite a gentleman,' said his wife. 'I think maybe you're prejudiced against him because he's an Easterner playing at ranching.'

'You women!' exploded Nat. 'Playin's right. Wal, he ain't gonna play with my daughter. Ef'n . . . '

'Oh, shush, don't be so melodramatic,' said Mrs Hodgeson.

Jack Sharp was pretty certain now of what had happened to his pard but he kept silent about it.

Hank Bulger drove up in his buggy with another of the Horse V rannies on the seat beside him.

'You got your hoss, Jack?' he said. 'Or d'yuh want a lift?'

'I've got my hoss, thanks, Boss.'

'Wal, what yuh hangin' about there for?'

The Old Man's thoughts for the welfare of his boys, and the questions that went with them were a bit trying at times.

Jack said: 'I'm waitin' for Mert.'

'Oh. Where's *he* gone?'

'I dunno.'

'Wal, mebbe he's gone home without yuh. You ain't his nuss-maid air yuh? Altho' I'll admit he needs one sometimes. He's probably got his feet up in the bunkhouse right now.'

'Maybe he has, the skunk,' said Jack. 'I'll be comin' right behind yuh, Boss.'

The Old Man looked at the Hodgesons. He wouldn't be so impertinent as to ask them why they lingered, but he was plainly desirous of knowing.

Nat said: 'You ain't seen Judy have yuh, Hank?'

The Old Man shook his white head. 'Nope.' Then he looked sharply at Jack. 'Has Mert gone off with Judy?'

'No, Boss, the two of 'em ain't very friendly lately.'

'Humph!'

'We hear that Judy rode out with Colly Johnson,' said Mrs Hodgeson.

'Oh,' said Hank. 'Wal you ain't got anything to worry about then. She won't come tuh no harm from that milksop . . . ' The Old Man paused. Then he looked at Jack again. He was very shrewd. Nothing much that went on missed his eyes. 'Mebbe you'd better mosey over to the Double W,' he said.

'I'll do that,' said Jack. He was glad the Old Man had made the decision for him. He forked his horse and thundered off. He knew the Double W boys who had been present at the barbecue had gone in front of him. He wasn't likely to meet anybody on the trail, but he didn't want to go crashing into the Double W spread on a wild goose chase and maybe stop a bullet from a nervous night rider. As he got nearer to the big ranch which was ablaze with light, he slowed his horse to a trot, and as was his custom in a ticklish situation, began to think things out beforehand.

Again the decision was taken out of his hands: a bunch of horsemen thundered towards him. He jogged his horse forward to meet them. They surrounded him, their attitudes inclined to be menacing. They were all Double W men, and led, it seemed, by a character who was known as 'Bronc' Malone. He spoke: 'Where yuh headin', Jack?' His voice had a curious timbre.

Jack had a sudden foreboding that almost stifled him. He couldn't find words for a moment as the hostile group watched him and waited. He decided that the truth was the best. He said: — 'I'm lookin' f'r my pard, Mert Scanlon.'

'So are we,' said Malone. 'Johnson's daid an' Ruston's got a busted shoulder. All the work o' that hellion pard o' yourn. When we catch him we're gonna string him higher'n a kite.'

'There must be some mistake . . . '

'There's no mistake,' said Malone harshly. 'Ruston saw Scanlon shoot the boss. Then he turned an' shot Ruston. Brad's lucky he ain't daid. The Hodgeson gel was there too. Her an' Scanlon lit out together.'

'Wait a minute,' yelled one of the men suddenly. 'What's he doin' here anyway? How did he know his pard 'ud be up this way . . . '

'Yeah,' said somebody else. 'Mebbe he had somep'n tuh do with it.'

Jack's clear voice broke into the babble.

'I wuz lookin' f'r Mert, knowing he wouldn't ride home without me. Somebody told me they saw him coming this way . . . ' He knew that what Bronc Malone had said was true. Johnson was dead. Ruston had a busted shoulder and Mert was mixed up in it — and Judy. He was not surprised. He had known something like this would have to happen sooner or later. He said:

'If Mert did any shootin', it'd be in self-defence . . . '

'Johnson never had a chance,' said the harsh-voiced Malone. 'He seldom carried a gun. An' we didn't find one in the room . . . '

'Mert hadn't got his guns with him either,' said Jack. 'If he shot Johnson where did he get the gun?'

'What's the hagglin' about,' yelled a man.

Malone said: 'We're ridin' tuh the Horse V. You'd better come with us.' It was an order. Jack looked around him at the menacing figures in the darkness.

'Yeah, I guess I'd better,' he said.

They were silent then as they set off at a gallop. They soon ate up the couple of miles to the Horse V ranch house. The Old Man came running out to meet them.

'Let me tell him,' said Jack.

Malone nodded. He raised his hands as his men began to clamour.

'Let Mr Bulger's own boy tell it,' he said. 'If he tells it wrong we kin soon correct him.'

Jack dismounted and faced the Old Man, who stood silent, waiting for him to begin.

Swiftly, trying to keep his voice as level as possible, Jack told the Old Man all he had heard from the Double W boys. Hank's seamed face began to look older in the dim light, his eyes were shadowed.

When Jack had finished, he said, 'Has the sheriff been called in?'

'One o' the boys went after him,' said Malone.

'An' you all come rampaging on like wild men — no proof — no rights . . . '

'We aim tuh git Scanlon,' bawled one hothead. 'If he's here we want him.'

The Old Man got his dander up. 'He ain't here,' he retorted. 'I ain't seen him. An' if he was here I wouldn't turn him over tuh nobody but the law.'

'I'll betcha the skunk's hidin' in there,' said the same voice from the other side. 'Let's root him out.'

The Old Man said: 'I give yuh my word of honour that Mert Scanlon ain't hidin' here . . . Now get off my land. I'll talk tuh the law later.'

Men were coming from the bunk-house now, asking what was going on. A hostile group faced the Double W men.

'You cain't do nothin' here, Malone,

except start a peck o' trouble,' said Jack Sharp.

Bronc Malone saw that he was beaten. He began to shepherd his men away. As they went he threw one parting shot over his shoulder. 'If you're stringin' us along you'll pay f'r it later.'

His answer was a menacing growl from the Horse V men. Then the Double W riders were swallowed up in the night.

'It's a bad business,' said Hank Bulger, shaking his white head. 'D'you know where Mert is, Jack?'

'I wish I did.'

'An' young Judy — what's happened to her?'

The last question was answered a few minutes later when Mr and Mrs Hodgeson careered up in their buckboard, a white-faced girl on the seat between them.

They got down. 'Where is he?' said the Old Man immediately.

Nat Hodgeson shook his narrow,

greying head. 'We don't know. He left Judy. She came right home. She don't know where he wuz makin' for.'

'Was he comin' in this direction?' asked Jack Sharp.

'No,' said the girl softly. Then she began to tell her tale. Her voice trembled a little and she nervously clasped and unclasped her small white hands. Everybody listened in sympathetic silence.

She, being a very keen horsewoman, had shown interest in Johnson's latest acquisition, a pure-bred white Arabian colt. He had persuaded her to go along to the ranch and have a look at the horse. They went to the corral first and admired the magnificent animal. Then he asked her to go into the ranch house with him for supper, before he took her home. She declined, but he was very insistent, so she temporized by agreeing to go in with him and have a quick drink.

Up till then his manner had been very gentlemanly, quite above reproach, but once inside the ranch house, it changed. He had been drinking fairly heavily all night and now Judy realized it had had more effect on him than she had thought. He began to make advances and when she avoided them, he became aggressive. It was then that Mert Scanlon burst in.

'They fought terribly,' said Judy. 'I ran for help and met Brad Ruston. When we got back to the room they were wrestling for a gun. Johnson seemed to have it in his hand. Then it went off and he fell. Ruston shot at Mert and missed. Mert shot back with the gun he had picked from the floor and hit Ruston in the shoulder.'

'What kind of a gun was it, Judy?' asked Jack Sharp.

'It wasn't a Colt. It was a smaller one, thirty-eight calibre I think.'

'Mert didn't take his guns with him,' said Jack. 'Anyway, he never owned a thirty-eight in his life. It must've been Johnson's gun that he pulled from somewhere. It wuz self-defence all

44

along the line. It wuz self-defence with Ruston too, wasn't it, Judy?'

'It was,' said the girl. 'Ruston meant to kill Mert.'

'What happened after Ruston got hit?' asked the Old Man.

'Mert picked up both guns. We left the ranch together.'

'That was a mistake tuh take the guns,' said the Old Man. 'Ruston didn't say it wuz self-defence. It's his word agin yours. This is gonna raise a stink that'll reach plumb across the County . . . '

'Mert was going to bring me home,' said the girl. 'But I was scared for him and made him leave me. I thought he'd come here.'

'He hasn't — leastways, nobody's seen him.'

'It's all my fault,' burst out the girl. 'If I hadn't gone with that beastly man . . . '

'Don't blame yourself,' said Jack Sharp. 'Somethin' like this had gotta happen tuh Mert sooner or later.' He strode forward. 'Come an' sit down, Judy.'

The girl let him lead her to a bench on the veranda of the ranchhouse. She was silent for a few moments, then she said: 'I thought nothing about Johnson. He was just an amusing companion. I went with him to show Mert that he wasn't the only man on the earth. He's so arrogant and intolerant at times and I wanted to teach him a lesson. Oh, if I'd only known how badly he felt about it . . . '

'You're kinda fond of him, ain't yuh?' said Jack softly.

'I am fond of him,' said the girl. 'But I've never given him any reason to think he had proprietory rights over me. An' that's the way he acted . . . But I was a fool! I shouldn't have gone with Johnson.' There was a little sob in her voice. 'If only I'd known. It's all my fault . . . '

'Easy, Judy,' said Jack. 'Easy.' He put a brotherly arm around her slim shoulders. 'You couldn't know, it's silly

46

to blame yourself.'

'Yes, I suppose it is,' said the girl. Then, softly, 'You're a good friend to Mert, Jack.'

'That's what he needs right now,' said the cowboy grimly. 'Plenty of good friends.'

3

'Born For Trouble'

The Hodgesons left the Horse V. The next arrival was expected, but not wholly welcome. It was the lean, sour-faced sheriff of San Martini, Ep Blackson. With him was a posse from town and Bronc Malone and the boys from the Double W — quite a sizeable bunch all told.

'Where's that murderin' young skunk, Scanlon?' was the sheriff's greeting.

'Whatever Mert Scanlon did, it wasn't murder,' retorted the Old Man. 'An' if you catch him you'll have tuh prove it.'

'We'll catch him,' said Blackson. 'Fust of all we gotta search this place.'

'You're the law,' said the Old Man, ironically. 'An' I believe in law and order. Carry on with your searchin', but be careful . . . The law, I said!' he barked, as Bronc Malone started forward. 'You Double W men stay where you are.'

'I don't like your attitude,' snarled Malone.

'You ain't intended to.'

Watched at every point by hostile cowboys, the sheriff and his posse began their search. Needless to say they did not find Mert Scanlon.

'Like I said,' the Old Man told them. 'Mert ain't here. As far as I know he ain't been here since the barbecue.'

'You're glad about it,' accused the sheriff.

'Suttinly I'm glad about it!' Then the Old Man went on a new tack. 'Have yuh seen Miss Judy?'

'No.'

'Wal, mebbe you'd better see her. Mebbe ef'n yuh do, you'll figure Johnson only got what he asked for.'

'No matter how you look at it, it's cold-blooded murder,' said the sheriff.

'An' I won't rest until I get the skunk. This is a fine advertisement for Western hospitality, ain't it? It'll raise hell from here to Chicago.' He wheeled his horse. 'Come on, let's git goin'.'

The bunch thundered away. The Old Man said: 'I'm all f'r law an' order an' I ain't condoning what young Mert done. He wuz born for trouble that younker was. He was bound to raise hell sooner or later, but that pesky skinflint of a lawman gits in my craw.'

The Horse V boys milled around. Some of them suggested going after the posse to see that Mert got a square deal if they caught him.

'The sheriff ain't that bad,' said the Old Man. 'He'll see that Mert don't come to no harm an' gets clapped into a cell. A feather in his cap f'r him. He ain't handled a real killer for years.'

'I'm thinkin' Mert ain't likely to be caught,' said Jack.

'Mebbe he'd be better tuh give hisself up,' said old Hank. 'An' fight it out that way. We'd back him tuh the last man — wouldn't we, boys?'

'Sure . . . Sure!'

'I guess his mistake wuz runnin' away in the fust place,' said Jack. 'But any of us 'ud've done the same.'

'Mebbe he means tuh come back when the hue an' cry dies down.' said another hand. 'The way those Double W boys air now they're liable to shoot him on sight . . . '

'Aw, what's the use of talkin'?' said Jack with a savage vehemence that was unusual for him. 'We cain't do nothin' about it right now. We don't know where Mert is. We might never see him again. We cain't do nothin' a'tall.'

For all its vehemence, there was sense in that statement. The boys began to drift to the bunkhouse. It was very late and many of them were still carrying a bellyful of liquor.

The Old Man said wearily: 'Wal, we must hope f'r the best.' Then he went.

Jack Sharp was left alone. He rolled a cigarette, lit it, then moseyed over to the corral. He wished he could do something to help his pard; but he had no lead, nothing at all to go on. He leaned on a corner-post of the corral fence in the shadow of an old feed-barn.

It was about 2 a.m. The night was dark and still, with a warm, very slight breeze. Jack stood in a black pool of shadow and looked out into the night, but visibility was very poor. Jack was glad of that. It gave Mert a better chance anyway.

The man came from the feed-barn and was almost at his elbow before Jack became aware of his presence. He whirled.

'All right, pardner,' said a well-known voice.

'Mert! Gosh, I never expected tuh see you here. Where've yuh been?'

'Burrowing into a pile of straw like a scared rat,' said the tall cowboy. There was a bitter note in his voice. 'I wuz there when the posse searched. I didn't mean tuh leave without sayin' so-long to yuh.'

'You'll hafta get goin',' said Jack urgently. 'They're all around lookin' f'r yuh.'

'I've fooled 'em once, I'll fool 'em again,' said Mert. 'I had tuh kill Johnson, Jack. It wuz self-defence; and the same with Ruston. He tried to kill me.'

'Yeah, I know,' said Jack. 'Don't you worry about that. I'll get my hoss — I'm comin' with yuh.'

'No you're not,' said Mert. 'There's no need f'r you to get dragged into it . . . I'll tell yuh where you can get in touch with me.'

'The Ol' Man said maybe if you give yourself up . . . '

'An' get myself crucified? Yuh know I wouldn't do that.'

'I guess not,' said Jack. Then: 'Where's your hoss? How . . . ?'

'He's in the stable wi' the rest of 'em. Unsaddled and rubbed-down. They weren't lookin' for him so they didn't notice him.'

'By Cracky!' said Jack. 'That was

smart. Come on . . . Watch your step.'

They reached the stables without mishap and Jack helped Mert to saddle his mount. Then he began to saddle his own.

'There's no need f'r that I told yuh,' said Mert. 'You can help me more by stayin' here. I'm gonna hole up in the old line-hut by the Jelly Buttes. There's a cellar under there if yuh remember — leads right intuh the ol' mine. Allus a good getaway. If yuh can bring me food an' news from time tuh time . . . I ain't gonna leave this territory without a fight . . . '

Finally, Jack was persuaded to stay. He watched Mert ride away until he was swallowed up in the blackness.

Mert rode slowly, keeping to the long grass which deadened the sound of his horse's hoofs. Maybe he ought to have lit out an hour ago when he had a better chance. He could not analyse the perverse reasons that made him return to the Horse V. He had never meant to stop and face the music anyway. And he had not only returned just to see Jack. Maybe it was just because he liked taking risks, living dangerously. Was that what he was made for? He felt no fear now, but rather a strange exultation. He was a hunted outlaw and he felt almost happy.

The breeze was cooler now, blowing from the slopes above. He kneed his horse to a faster pace. Then suddenly a horseman loomed up out of the darkness.

A voice said: 'Hold it.' Then the two riders came face to face and the voice spoke again: 'Scanlon!'

A stab of flame blossomed from Mert's hip. The crash of the shot echoed and re-echoed in the night. The other rider swayed in the saddle then tumbled headlong, to be almost swallowed in the long grass. The riderless horse snorted in terror, swerved past Mert's mount and galloped off. The tall cowboy kicked his mount savagely in the ribs and it bounded forward. The wind whipped at them as the horse galloped at break-neck speed.

Jack Sharp heard the shot. It did not sound far away. He began to run in the direction from which it came. Light blazed in the ranch house behind him and he heard voices. Some of the boys were alert once more.

As he ran, his heart thudded in his chest. He had that stifling sense of foreboding again.

The riderless horse careered suddenly out of the darkness, nearly knocking him down, and galloped on. Jack did not have a chance to have a good look at it. He hoped it wasn't Mert's mount.

He paused. Somewhere round here the shot must have been fired. He thought he heard hoofs drumming away in front, far in the distance. Then he saw the shape half-hidden in the long grass. It looked like a log — but Jack knew it was not that.

He went down on his knees beside the man. He heard the boys coming nearer and shouted: 'Here! Over here!'

There was an answering hail.

The man lay still on his face. Jack rolled him over. It was not Mert he was pretty sure of that. He thought that maybe it would be better if it was Mert. He struck a match.

The flame spluttered then blossomed, illuminating, with sickening clarity, the face of Pete Jilson, one of Sheriff Blackson's deputies. The lean brown features were marred by a spreading red stain which seemed to start at a point on the bridge of Jilson's nose. There was a horrible glazed look of surprise in the sightless eyes. The match went out.

Two more Horse V boys joined Jack.

'Who is it?' said one.

Jack told them. 'He's purty dead.' His own voice was dead too. He did not mean to sound callous.

'Who did it?'

'Mert I guess. He's bin here . . . '

'Mert — where? How . . . ?'

Jack struck another match. He touched the dead man's wrist and the

57

gun that lay in the lax fingers.

'It seems like the sheriff left some-body tuh keep watch jest in case — Mert wuz hidin' in the ol' feed-barn all the time. I didn't know. He came out, said so-long, then he lit out. This *hombre* must've tried to stop him. Mert beat him to it . . . An' he made sure.'

'He made sure f'r himself too,' said one cowboy softly. 'He's suttinly burnt all his boats behind him now.'

★   ★   ★

Riding hard, the tall rider neither knew nor cared whether the man he had shot was dead. He rode like a man with a devil inside him, but with a definite objective in mind. It gave him sardonic satisfaction to know that somewhere in front of him were his hunters. And they would have been flabbergasted had they known their quarry was behind them. But he had to go wary. From time to time he stopped his horse and remained immobile for a moment — listening.

One time he thought he heard hoofbeats in the distance. He began to make a detour. A mile or so in front of him was a small range of hills, the furthermost end of the Horse V range. That was his destination. But maybe the posse was already searching up there.

If the hoofbeats had belonged to them, he neither saw them nor heard them again. He reached the hills by a circuitous route and began to climb, then descended again. He had made a small error of judgment — it was years since he had explored this region. Finally, however, he discovered the spot he sought.

He dismounted from his horse and led it forward. Next moment both of them disappeared as if the earth had opened up and swallowed them.

Once inside the old mine tunnel, Mert pulled the creepers back over the opening to conceal it. He spoke softly to his horse, gentling him with his hands. He struck a match which lit the walls of the tunnel, eerie, black and dripping with moisture. The air was cold down here, conditioned by hidden vents, fissures in the rocks above. Only the old men of the district knew of the existence of this disused place. Hank Bulger knew. So did Nat Hodgeson. Mert knew they would not talk. He had to take a chance that nobody else knew. He and Jack had stumbled on it while hunting up there one day. Little did they realize then the use to which it would be put by one of them.

Treading warily, Mert led the horse forward. He lit matches from time to time. The horse was quieter now. It had become used to the place.

Finally the tunnel widened to a dirt-floored cave which was dryer and warmer.

Mert lit a match and held it aloft.

'This'll do you for a bit, old timer,' he said. 'I'll get yuh some straw.'

He left the horse there. Perversely, his callousness with humans did not extend to dumb beasts. He climbed uneven steps hewn in the rock. He reached the top and pushed at the rock ceiling above him. With a protesting groan it began to shift; a whole section of it moving upwards and aside like a trapdoor. Mert climbed through.

The tall cowboy knew he was now in the most outlying Horse V line-hut on the edge of the Jelly Buttes. In the past, hundreds of night-riders had slept there, never dreaming that they lay over the exit of the old mine. The hut was originally built by three old prospectors who had discovered the bonanza, worked it until it petered out then, after the manner of their kind, hit the trail once more in search of the elusive rainbow which they seldom found this side of The Divide.

Mert pulled the piece of old sacking across the window, then he lit a match and peered around him. Three matches blazed and flickered out before he found what he sought: a stump of candle protruding from an old tin can.

After several attempts he managed to

light it. The flickering flame lit the cabin fitfully, throwing grotesque shadows on the dusty log walls and the few sticks of broken furniture; the rickety bunk with its tumbled moth-eaten blankets, the large packing case that served as a table, and two smaller boxes for chairs.

Mert went outside to see if any light showed through the improvized blind. There was a thin sliver at the side. He put that right, then began to gather dried grass for his horse.

He took this down into the cave, then removed his bandanna, wet it from his canteen and laved out the horse's mouth.

'That's all I kin spare yuh I'm afraid ol' timer,' he said. He took a swig himself. That would have to do him for tonight.

Anyway, he'd had plenty to eat and drink at the barbecue. That seemed ages ago: so much had happened since. He shut it from his mind.

He laid his saddle and horse-blanket

on the floor, blew out the candle and lay down.

Suddenly he rose again and dragged the huge packing-case table across against the door. He was pretty certain to wake if anybody approached the hut, but there was nothing like making sure. He had left the trap beneath the bunk slightly open, ready for a quick getaway if need be. He could hear his horse moving about down there. A faint smell arose: hay, horseflesh, musty air. With this in his nostrils he drifted into sleep. It was all so familiar. He might have been in the Horse V bunkhouse.

When he awoke it was lighter in the hut. He rose stiffly, crossed to the window, and raised the blind a little. Morning sunlight made him blink his eyes. He felt miserable, and devilishly hungry. That was what got a man down — hunger.

He rolled himself a cigarette. It was a good job he still had a sizeable sack of baccy and plenty of paper.

He smoked three cigarettes in quick

succession. They made him feel kind of sick. He checked over his guns, then rose and crossed to the door. He moved aside the big packing case and opened the door, cautiously venturing out into the sunlight.

It was a clear summer morning. Too early yet for the usual heat-haze to cloud visibility, and Mert could see to the horizon of the seemingly limitless mesa. The blue sky above was flawless.

He leaned against the already sun-warmed log walls of the cabin and rolled himself another cigarette.

He was smoking it when he saw a rapidly growing speck in the distance. He flipped the half-smoked weed away from him and backed into the cabin. Through the crack of the slightly open door he watched the rider approaching. It was Jack Sharp. He slowed his horse down as he came nearer, looking about him all the time.

Mert called him softly from the doorway. The freckle-faced cowboy acknowledged the greeting with a jerk of his head then rode his horse round to the back of the cabin. When he returned he was on foot. Mert opened the door wider and his pard stepped inside the cabin. He put a parcel on the packing-case table.

'Plenty o' chow there,' he said. 'An' a bottle o' lime-water an' a bottle o' whiskey.'

'Thanks,' said Mert. He began to open the parcel.

Jack said: 'I shouldn't figure on makin' a permanent hideout o' this place if I wuz you, Mert. Every available man in the territory is searching f'r yuh. An' nearly everybody's volunteered — except our own boys o' course.'

'So,' said Mert. 'Did yuh tell anybody where I wuz?'

'Nope. Not even the Old Man. I figured he'd want tuh turn yuh in an' see you stand trial now — after what happened early this mornin'.'

'That *hombre* I shot?'

'Yeah. It wuz Pete Jilson, the deppity.

He's daid. Pity yuh had tuh kill him, Mert. The pore cuss was only doin' his duty.'

'It was him or me.'

'Yeah, I guess so,' said Jack. 'Still, it's a pity he's daid — f'r both of yuh I guess.'

'It was him or me I tell yuh,' repeated Mert. He was like a child losing his temper now. 'Air yuh fer me or agin me, Jack?'

'I'm for yuh, pard,' said Jack. 'You hadn't oughta ask. But I don't hafta blow trumpets every time I see yuh do I? I'm advisin' yuh to light out from here as soon as possible. You're in a ticklish position. They're liable to stumble on yuh any time. An' even if you got out the back way you might bump into another bunch in the hills. They're out now — I had to come very careful to avoid them. F'r Pete's sake, Mert, get right away while you've still got a chance; there's bin enough shootin' . . . '

'Air yuh frightened somebody else

might get hurt?' said Mert sardonically. 'Some other poor innocent of a lynch-minded manhunter?'

Jack matched this with a shaft of his own. 'I shouldn't like to see you get your hide full o' lead no more'n anybody else.' Then his voice became metallic. ''Tain't no use me an' you jibing at each other . . . I've never steered yuh wrong before, have I?'

'Nope. I kin say that.'

'All right then. I'm tellin' yuh tuh go right now. An' I'll come with yuh if you want me to.'

'I've told yuh there's no need f'r you to get dragged into it a'tall,' said Mert. 'An' as f'r ridin' . . . Wal, I'll think about it'

Jack shrugged. 'Suit y'rself, pard,' he said. 'I gotta ride now. Folks get suspicious if I'm away too long. I'll be back. If you decide on ridin', wait for me . . . Tonight'

'All right,' said Mert.

4

'Adios, Amigo'

When Jack got back to the ranch, the Old Man was awaiting him.

'Where've yuh bin?' he demanded.

The cowboy's mind was not working on excuses. For once he was nonplussed. He said lamely: 'I jest bin out a piece, boss. Kind'a lookin'.'

'Kind'a lookin',' sneered Hank. A suspicious light came into his sharp, grey eyes.

'You've bin lookin' f'r that good-fernothin' pard of yourn.'

'Yeah,' admitted Jack.

'An' did yuh find him?'

'Nope,' lied the cowboy. 'He's probably a helluva lot of miles away by now.'

'The further the better I guess,' said the Old Man. 'I guess even now I kind of hope he gets away — although he don't deserve to.' He recollected himself and ceased his ruminations. He barked: 'When I want my top hands in a mornin', I expect 'em to be on the spot — not gallivantin' off on their lonesome. You gotta take two o' the boys out into Satan's Brush, lookin' fer strays. You know it better'n anybody. Pick any two you like. Git goin'.'

'Right, boss.' Jack was glad to get out of range of the Old Man's gimlet eyes.

He chose a couple of hardbitten rannies, pardners, known as Arizona and Gyp. They took a day's supply of chow and plenty of water and set out for the badlands, the waste of sand, cacti and sagebrush, an abortion of the lush mesa, known as Satan's Brush. Periodical sorties had to be made in this territory to comb it for stray dogies which, if not found in time, invariably went mad trying to find a way out of the prickly, heat distorted maze until finally they collapsed from wounds and exhaustion and died there.

The three men did not talk much and strangely enough, they shied away from the subject of Mert Scanlon. They were on the edge of the sagebrush when the first incident happened that was to remind them of him once more — and forcibly. It was hardly an incident really; only the fact that the keen-eyed Arizona looked back and spotted the bunch of horsemen that were coming fast behind them.

'Company,' he said laconically. 'In an all-fired hurry too.'

'Wal,' said Gyp. 'They kin soon ketch us up ef'n they want us. We ain't goin' no faster'n pesky mud-turtles.'

Jack Sharp looked back and said nothing but he thought about Mert Scanlon. Right now, so many things reminded him of Mert. He wondered if these galloping riders were bringing the news that Mert had been caught. Maybe he was dead now . . .

'It's Sheriff Blackson an' some of his boys,' said Arizona.

The new arrivals reined in, and

formed a half-circle around the three cowhands.

The Sheriff said: 'It's you three is it?'

'Nothin' but,' said Gyp jocularly.

'We didn't know there was any of yuh out this far,' said the sheriff. 'I suppose it's no use askin' yuh if you seen any signs of that killer we're huntin' 'cos, bein' pards of his, you wouldn't tell us if you had.'

'A man who answers his own questions allus saves other people a lotta trouble,' said Gyp. Dark, small, volatile, he was an inveterate wag.

But the sheriff was not listening. He was looking at Jack.

'I've bin wantin' tuh have a good talk with you, Jack,' he said.

'Wal, now's your chance, Sheriff.'

'Did you know Mert Scanlon was hidin' around the Hoss V last night?'

'No,' said Jack truthfully.

'You wuz the one who found the deputy right after he wuz shot — an' you said Scanlon had done it.' So the boys had talked, thought Jack grimly.

71

He said: 'I saw him making a run for it. At least it looked like him. Who else could it've bin anyway? The deputy wouldn't've pulled a gun on anybody else.'

Another man pushed his horse forward to the front of the group. Jack looked up into the square, scowling face of Bronc Malone. Malone said: 'You helped Scanlon get away. You're almost as much tuh blame f'r the deppity's death as he is.'

'You seem tuh have it in f'r me, Malone,' said Jack levelly. 'Why?'

'Why?' sneered Malone. 'You're the little innocent ain't yuh. You're Scanlon's best friend. Thick as thieves with him you are — probably know where he is right now. You knew where he'd gone last night. You came right after him. You probably knew what he meant to do all the time. You helped him hide at the ranch and helped him tuh get away. You helped him to kill that deppity.'

Jack was easy-going. But there were some things no man could back down to. He slid from the saddle and stood on his feet. Watching him, his two boys knew one thing, if Malone did not. Up till now Jack Sharp had been proved the fastest gunman in the territory — ever since he beat 'breed Joe Lopez to the draw and shot him dead in the Golden Pesos. Did Malone think he could haze him?

Malone dismounted. The two men faced each other on that stretch of greensward at the end of the badlands. They both crouched a little, watching each other closely. They did not see Sheriff Blackson's movements.

He barked: 'All right. The first man who goes for his gun gets plugged by me.'

Both men looked up into the muzzles of a twin pair of forty-fives — and the sheriff was notoriously trigger-happy.

'Sheriff,' said Bronc Malone. 'I demand you arrest this man. We'll get no place while he's around ready to slip away an' give his pard the news.'

Maybe the same thought was in the

lawman's mind, but he was not going to let the Double W man tell him his business.

He snarled: 'I'll run this my way, Bronc. Git back on your hoss, we can't haggle all day.'

The big waddy's eyes flamed as he turned back to his horse. As the sheriff holstered his guns, Malone turned suddenly and flung himself at Jack who was taken completely unawares. Malone's heavy weight and flailing fists bore him to the ground.

'Stop it!' yelled the sheriff, but the two men rolling in the dust paid him no heed.

Malone was too savage, too eager. Some of his blows hit the man beneath him, others smashed into the ground. The big man's fists suffered more than anything else. Dazed for a moment, Jack struck out mechanically, and Malone grunted as a lucky jab almost knocked his teeth down his throat. His own blow was deflected and went wide, then Jack was wide enough awake to dodge the next one, rolling his head to one side so that Malon's fist only grazed his temple. The Horse V man arched his knees, bringing them up as hard as he could into the small of his opponent's back. Kicking, Malone was catapulted over his head. The nails of his heavy riding boot cut a gash in Jack's forehead, bringing a splash of warm blood.

Jack was on his knees as Malone turned, and launched himself forward, but Malone was faster than he looked. He squirmed to one side. Missing his mark, Jack landed on all fours. He rose, turning swiftly to meet the big man's onslaught. He parried a left and received a right to the shoulder, tottering a bit. Over-eager once more, Malone came in too close and Jack got under his guard, sinking a right to his thick middle. Malone grunted and doubled up. Jack tried to uppercut him, but Malone was no novice. Though he was in pain he kept his chin tucked in. In desperation he brought his rock-like fist over. It crashed into the middle of Jack's back, driving him to his knees . . .

The horsemen were shouting encouragement to their particular favourite now. Powerless, the sour-faced sheriff looked on.

When Jack rose again, Malone was still gasping for breath, drawing it in with great, wheezing grunts. He shuffled away as the Horse V man advanced. They circled warily, then Jack sprang. Malone parried the shooting fists with a clever scissors-smother — he was a bruiser was this man, but Jack was the faster of the two: he swung suddenly to one side and attacked again. Malone turned to meet this sly onslaught and a fist exploded on his right ear, bringing fire-crackers to his brain. His guard went up a little too high then. Jack hit him in the solar-plexus. The big man's breath went from him in an agonized sigh, tottering backwards, still trying to cover up.

Jack followed him up, throwing blows

from all angles, punishing him unmercifully. Malone backed into his horse's flanks. He seemed to be sinking. Jack stepped away from him.

Suddenly, Malone seemed to rally. Then, like a sidewinder striking, he went for his gun. Jack, wiping blood from his forehead with his sleeve, was helpless. The shot came from behind him. Malone gave a cry of agony and the gun spun from his hand, flashed in the sunlight and hit the ground with a dull thud. The Double W man cursed luridly and nursed his throbbing fingers.

Smoke curled lazily from the muzzle of the Colt in Arizona's hand. The sheriff had his gun out too, now. The lawman and the red-headed Horse V man looked at each other. Death leered over both their shoulders.

The sheriff was trigger-happy, but he was also sensible. He said:

'All right, Arizona, put way your iron. I guess Malone asked f'r it.'

Both men holstered their guns. Jack

turned. 'Thanks, Arizony,' he said.

'Don't mention it, pardner.'

'Git up your hoss, Bronc,' said the sheriff.

Scowling hate in all directions, the big Double W waddy did as he was told.

The sheriff turned his horse. He threw one last glance back at Jack Sharp. 'Watch yourself, Jack,' he said cryptically. Then the whole bunch of them thundered off.

'Ah, me,' said little Gyp. 'Trouble an' strife. Forward, men.' The trio pushed on into Satan's Brush.

They found a calf that, blundering in panic, had impaled itself on the cruel spikes of a cholla cactus. It was still struggling weakly and bleating softly like a sick child. Jack put a bullet through its brain. The carcase was irretrievable; they had to leave it for the buzzards.

Deeper in the sun-tortured maze, with the fantastic plant-life which clutched and scratched at them with hungry fingers, they found another carcase, already half-eaten. Wheeling buzzards scolded them shrilly from above.

Then they heard a more pitiful mooing and a dogie tottered towards them and stood trembling. Jack took off his hat and tipped a measure of water into it from his canteen. He dismounted and advanced on the dogie. The beast shied away from him. Jack laid the hat on the sand and retreated once more.

The dogie came forward again cautiously, circling the mysterious dirty brown thing. But the smell of water was too strong for it; it conquered its timidity. It made a little plunge and dipped its nose in the hat.

The red-headed Arizona took his riata from his saddle-horn and neatly looped the beast.

'Take him out on grass,' said Jack. 'Give him another drink before you leave him.'

The orders were needless: all three

men knew their jobs too well, but talking broke the spell of the hot, still, monotony. Arizona led the stray away.

Suddenly he called back: 'Boys. Another one here.'

'Gettin' quite a bag today ain't we?' said little Gyp.

They joined Arizona. Another calf staggered in front of them, its tongue lolling out, its eyes bulging. Again Jack dismounted and repeated the process with the hat and the water. The calf revived miraculously.

'Tough little crittur ain't he?' said Arizona as he added the little piebald beast to his string.

To the right of them, squealing buzzards were plummetting like stones from the sky to squabble around the carcase on the cholla cactus.

Gyp raised his rifle. Through constant practise he was a crack shot. He fired. A descending buzzard paused in mid-air, then dropped again, a heap of tangled feathers.

The cartridge case spun in the

sunlight. Gyp fired again into a rising bunch of them. Another one tumbled to the ground, then, screeching and complaining, the buzzards wheeled away from their meal. Gyp chuckled.

'Nice shootin',' said Jack.

Arizona returned and they continued to search. When they stopped for chow, lying in what little shade they could find beneath a gnarled pulpy mass of fungi, they had found no more strays.

In the afternoon they found three more, one dead from thirst. The buzzards rose in a small cloud from the carcase, leaving it exposed to the sun and the flies.

When the trio started back for home, twilight was purpling the sky. They left Satan's Bush behind them like a fantastic nightmare.

★ ★ ★

After chow, Jack Sharp went outside for a smoke. It was another dark night. He took his usual stand by the corner of the corral, in the black shade of the old feed-barn. It was very quiet here.

He flipped away the stub of his cigarette and went round the back of the barn. He skirted the ranch-buildings. From the bunkhouse came the sound of laughter. He went along the backs of the places without meeting a soul, then reached his objective, the back of the cookhouse.

The cookhouse was in darkness. Sam, the mulatto cook, was probably playing poker with the boys in the bunkhouse, which was connected to his lean-to by a single, rickety door. Looking through the window, Jack could see the shaft of light coming from beneath the door and slashing a narrow path across the blackness of the cookhouse.

He opened the door and slid through. He tiptoed to the communicating door and listened. He could hear voices plainly through the thin partition. He listened for Sam's. Finally he heard it. He was safe in there all right and with a good hand by the sound of things.

Jack began to work fast. This was not the first time he had raided the kitchen, but never before in such suspicious circumstances. He knew his way around, and pretty soon had all the stuff he wanted stashed up in an old flour sack. He left the place as silently as he had entered it.

He went to the stable and saddled his horse, then, riding slowly and cautiously at first, set out. Once out of earshot of the ranch buildings he set his mount at a gallop. At one point he had to make a wide detour to avoid the herd and the sharp-eared night-riders.

He reached the Jelly Buttes and cautiously approached the old line-cabin. There was no answer to his soft hail. He paused. Was that hoofbeats he heard in the distance? No — probably a trick of the wind. He left his horse and, gun in hand, advanced on the cabin.

He kicked the door open, but stayed outside, pressed against the log wall beside it. There was no sound from inside. Maybe Mert was down in the passage . . . Jack went inside the cabin. He listened again.

He closed the door behind him and made sure the sacking-curtain was up at the window. Then he lit the stump of candle in the tin can. He took it over by the bunk and placed it on the floor. He lifted up the boards that concealed the secret exit and lowered himself down to the steps below. He reached out and got the candle, then closed the trap behind him.

Down here there was a stable-like smell, and dead silence. Jack held the candle aloft. He saw the straw where the horse had been. In the middle of it was a small boulder. Beside it something gleamed white. Jack crossed the cavern and went down on his knees in the straw.

Pinned beneath the boulder was a sheet of white paper, words pencilled on it in block capitals. Jack bent nearer and read them aloud.

I HAVE TAKEN YOUR ADVICE AND
AM LEAVING THE TERRITORY —
ADIOS AMIGO.

Jack tore the paper loose, screwed it
into a ball and absent-mindedly tucked
it into his vest-pocket.

'Wal — that's that,' he said softly. But
he was kind of hurt that Mert had not
waited for him. Anyway he had made
sure the note gave nothing away if
anybody else found it. Jack figured
maybe he would hear some more later.

He went up the steps and lifted the
trapdoor. Poking his head out, he felt a
draught of air and the flame of the
candle flickered and went out. The
cabin door was open.

Jack cursed and climbed out from
under the bunk. Then he went for his
gun. There was a quick scrape of feet,
something cold and hard hit him on the
back of the head. He collapsed to his
knees, shaking his head, trying to fight.
But sickness and blackness overcame
him. He sank lower and from far, far

away he heard a strangely familiar voice say:

'Stay still or I'll let you have it.'

When Jack raised his head again, the sickly light of the candle stabbing his aching eyeballs, there seemed to be a forest of thick legs all around. He clutched hold of the big packing-case and levered himself to his feet.

Faces floated around him like yellow blobs of grease in muddy soup. Then one of them moved a little nearer than the others and the features began to come into focus.

The harsh voice completed the sudden picture as it said: 'So this is the little hidey-hole is it?' It belonged to Bronc Malone. The Double W waddy's big, square face leered at Jack. It still bore the marks of the freckle-faced cowboy's fists.

Malone had four other Double W men with him. They seemed to fill the little hut and they all held guns.

'Where's Scanlon?' said Malone.

'I don't know,' said Jack.

'Joe, Blackie — get down through the trap.'

The two Double W men hesitated a mite. They did not seem keen to venture into the darkness below.

'Git goin'!' Malone scowled murderously.

Joe and Blackie lowered themselves into the black maw and disappeared from sight.

'I'm askin' yuh again,' said Malone. 'Where's Scanlon?'

Jack felt stronger now. His head was only an irritating throb. He wanted to smash Malone's face again.

He said: 'I've told yuh — I don't know!'

'You came here tuh see him didn't yuh?'

'I came here thinking he might be here,' said Jack. 'But he wasn't. I don't know where he is.'

'Yuh cain't lie your way out of it,' snarled Malone. He grabbed the bulging flour sack from the floor and upturned it on the packing-case table.

The groceries tumbled out. 'You wouldn't've brought this if you weren't purty sure Scanlon was here.'

'I brought it jest in case,' said Jack.

Malone was suddenly enraged by these calm commonplace answers. He started forward and swung his gun. Jack tried to duck, but wasn't quick enough. Bringing blinding pain, the gunbarrel tore a groove in the flesh from the cowboy's temple to the corner of his mouth. Swaying, Jack held on to the packing-case. A jagged red line made his face contorted and horrible. Blood dripped from his chin, staining his neckerchief and the breast of his shirt. His calmness had left him now. His grey eyes were murderous. Only the menace of the levelled guns held him still.

'You bastard!' he said. 'Someday I'll kill yuh for that.'

'Mebbe you won't get a chance to,' sneered Malone.

He spoke out of the corner of his mouth to one of the men. 'See what's keepin' them two.' Then as the man crossed the floor, Malone changed his mind. 'Wait a minute — we'll all go — jest in case Scanlon is skulkin' somewhere down there. Scanlon's little pard can go down first.' He jerked his gun. 'Git movin,' pard.'

Jack turned to lead the way. Maybe now he'd have a chance to get back at this big skunk. His hopes dropped a little as one of the men swung up behind him and relieved him of his guns: a precaution they evidently had not considered necessary until right now.

Jack dropped into the black hole, feeling for the steps with his feet. One of the Double W men came behind him carrying the candle.

They clustered in the cavern. From the passage up ahead a voice shouted: 'That you, Bronc?'

'Yuh damned fool,' bawled Malone. 'You'd be in a mess if it wasn't, wouldn't yuh?'

The two searchers loomed out of the blackness.

'This passage leads out intuh the hills,' said one. 'There ain't a sight o' nothin' or nobody.'

'He's got away all right,' said Malone. 'But he's bin here. There's bin a hoss here too. Over here — look. Git movin', Sharp.'

The man with the candle held it aloft above the straw.

'What's that boulder doin' here,' said Malone. 'Mebbe it's hidin' sump'n.'

He bent over to lift it. Then Jack Sharp acted. With a sweep of his arm he knocked the candle from the man's hand.

5

'Call Me George'

Warm velvet night blanketed San Antonio, dulling the edges of its myriad, blustering sounds. The clankety pianos in the honky-tonks, the guitars in the patios, the soft Mexican voices, the nasal American, the bellowing laughter, the screeching of the whores . . . High heeled riding-boots clacking on the boardwalk, horses' hoofs muffled in the dust of the road which choked men's throats and made their eyes smart . . . The creaking of saddle-leather, the jingling of harness, the rumble and rattle of waggon-wheels — the never-ceasing hum and babble of this cosmopolitan frontier-town, where the nasal-toned carpet-baggers and the lusty cowboys mingled with the twilight faces and soft mystery of Old Mexico.

Where the dim old temples stood cheek by jowl with the raw, garish gin-palaces, the dance-halls, the gambling hells and the brothels: and inscrutable Indians and dirty half-breeds moved like a creeping pestilence through the lusty mêlée.

San Antonio had a huge shifting population. Strangers came and went: gamblers, showmen, confidence-men of every kind, outlaws, desperadoes, the off-scourings of a young, growing civilization. There was a Texas Ranger post right there in the heart of it all. But these hardbitten trouble-shooters seldom interfered in town. There was a marshal and deputies who were supposed to look after that. The Lone-Star buckoes had a wider field. Their dour leader, Major Cliff Gaggo, was a diplomat. Let his boys raise their own private shennanigans in town, he saw that their assignments took them out of it. He'd sooner let a Wanted man leave San Antonio and pick him up some-where else than clap him in jail right here. It caused less trouble that way — and less killings.

Cowboys, coming in for a night's spree, rode their horses into the livery-stables, whose owners stood outside vying each other with their cajoling cries — although there was enough trade for all of them. But if one leather-voiced horse-handler could entice a grinning cowboy away from his neighbours' doors he was highly delighted.

One tall ranny who looked as if he'd been through a dust-bowl, and whose horse was on his last legs, ignored their blandishments. His face was dark, dirty, and had a black stubbly beard.

He halted finally at the door of Panhandle Jones's place round the corner from the Main Street. Panhandle was old; he liked peace and quiet. He had his regular customers so why should he bother to act like a cheap carpet-bagger. He came forward from the warm, smelly gloom of his stables as the travel-stained ranny led his horse in. Panhandle knew the look of that tall figure etched blackly in the doorway. He knew the horse too.

He said softly: 'Howdy, Mert.'

'Call me George,' said the other man. There was no humour in his deep voice.

'You're makin' quite a name for y'self ain't yuh — George?' said Panhandle. 'I dunno how you had the nerve to ride along the street of San Antonio.'

'Nobody 'ud expect tuh find me here. They'll all think I'm miles away from the territory now . . . Unless somebody tells 'em different.'

'Ef'n that sentence was meant 'specially for me, son,' said Panhandle. 'There was no need for it. Ef'n yuh thought that, you shouldn't've come here . . . You oughta know I wouldn't turn on yuh no matter what you done. I'm probably the only man alive who knew who your father was. An' you're probably the only man who knows that I rode the owlhoot trail with him. We're almost kin, boy.'

'Fergit it, ol'timer,' said Mert Scanlon. 'Whadyuh think I came here for?'

That question needed no answer. Panhandle said: 'Let's cut the gab. Get through intuh the kitchen. I'll see to your hoss.'

'Thanks,' said the cowboy. He passed the old man in the soft half-light and opened a door at the brighter end of the stables where a hurricane lantern hung on a hook in the wall. He passed into the kitchen of Panhandle's living quarters.

Although the night was warm, there was a small fire burning in the grate of the black cooking-range. The odour of warm food assailed Mert's nostrils, drifted into his empty stomach, making him feel weak and sick. He sunk a pitcher into the water-butt and drunk gratefully of the cool liquid. Then he slumped down in the old rocker and took his spurs and boots off. He divested himself of his dirty, embroidered vest and his gunbelt, which he hung over the back of the chair. He took off his dust-caked bandanna and his sweat-soaked sombrero and dropped them on the floor beside him. He opened wide the neck of his rough union-shirt, then with a sigh, like a man at the end of his tether, leaned back in the chair and closed his eyes.

He was alert in an instant when Panhandle entered the room, but the old man was alone. He closed the door behind him, and said: 'I'll get you some chow.'

Panhandle was a widower with no kin. He lived alone and did all his own cooking — and mighty fine it was too. Pretty soon he put a plate of beef, beans, potatoes and hot *frijoles* on the corner of the rough deal table.

'Draw up your chair, Mert,' he said. 'I'll make some coffee.'

The young man attacked the food wolfishly. When Panhandle put the cup of steaming coffee before him, he half-emptied it of the scalding liquid in one gulp. Tears came into his eyes and he began to splutter.

'Mite hasty that time weren't yuh, son,' said the old man.

He sat on the chair opposite and watched Mert finish his meal, then he rolled a cigarette across the table-top towards him. He clapped a battered clay pipe between his own pinched lips. They lit up. Mert blew smoke down his nostrils with luxurious content.

'This is the first smoke I've had all day,' he said. 'I lost my makings last night in a clump of prickly cacti on the edge of the badlands. A posse passed so close I could've spit on 'em . . . I've bin dodging ever since. I ain't let 'em see me. I think most of 'em are giving up now. They probably figure I'm at the other end o' the State or over the border or sump'n.'

'Pity you ain't over the border,' said Panhandle. 'You'd stand a better chance there.'

'They ain't makin' me run away with my tail between my legs,' said Mert harshly. 'I ain't aimin' tuh rot in the sun on the other side o' the Rio.'

'Every lawman in the State's on the lookout f'r yuh,' said Panhandle. 'Ol' Man Johnson has cabled from Chicago offering a reward of five thousand dollars for your capture. It ain't official yet — so far it's for lawmen only — seein' as they ain't had an inquest on the boy yet an' passed a verdict. Lemmy Buxton told me — in confidence sort of . . .'

'Lemmy Buxton, the ranger?'

'Who else?'

'Does he still come here?'

'From time tuh time. I saw him this mawnin'. Might not see him again for another week.'

'Does he know you know me?'

'I don't figure so. I don't think he knows you've ever bin in San Antonio. He's a decent cuss, Mert — as lawmen go.'

'I got nothin' agin him,' said Mert. 'But he'd better not get in my way.'

'Like that deppity,' said Panhandle.

Mert looked up at him sharply, his

temper showing in his unshaven face for a moment.

'I'd better tell yuh how the whole set-up was I guess,' he said. He began to talk, huskily.

When he had finished, Panhandle said: 'It was a bad break that started it, Mert. Yuh dad useter have bad breaks like that. He had a temper like you too . . . '

'I don't wanta hear about the ol' man,' interrupted Mert harshly.

'A temper like that,' said Panhandle. Then seeing the danger-lights in the young man's dark eyes, he shrugged his thin shoulders.

'All right . . . Like I wuz saying, it cain't be helped.' Then he said a phrase similar to one that had come from another oldtimer's lips not so long before: 'I guess you're just naturally made f'r trouble.'

Mert rose. 'I'll have a scrub-down,' he said. 'An' can I borrow your razor, ol' timer?'

'Sure yuh can.'

'Then I'd like to hideout in the loft for a mite.'

The old man hesitated for a fraction. He had not bargained for that. Then he said: 'All right, younker. Jest as you say. Mebbe you'll have a better chance when the hue an' cry's died down.'

'I got my reasons,' said Mert, but right then he did not say what they were.

He stripped to the waist. He was superbly built; his torso tapering from wide muscular shoulders to a slim waist and a flat, washboard middle. His chest was deep and sprinkled with fine black hairs. The muscles rippled beneath the dark velvety flesh.

Watching him lave his body with soap and water, old Panhandle suddenly felt a twinge of pity. He remembered, with a faint sadness, another young man who had looked so much like this one. Jack Gomez he had called himself. He was a border desperado who hated conventions and the law, and loved action and guns and women and horses

— and the open spaces beneath the sky. He and his band, who called themselves the Conquistadores, after the fabulous Spanish adventurers of that name, preyed on the landowners and travellers of the Rio Grande for two years or more. Gomez was a romantic figure; an educated man too, with a superb build, flowing jet-black hair, a curly moustache and an imperial which gave distinction to his hawk-like features. His men worshipped him — among them his right-hand man, a tow-headed beanpole named Chris Jones — it wasn't until years later, when the Conquistadores were only a bloody memory, that he became known as Panhandle.

Like many men of his ruthless and romantic nature, Jack Gomez's only weakness was women. He met up with a rancher's daughter, tawny-haired, fiery — the only woman who would not succumb easily to his charms. His pride wounded, this adventurer who had never previously loved anybody else but himself, conceived an overwhelming passion for this girl, whose name was Arabella. Finally he won her, but, to keep her, he married her and installed her in a log-castle on the fringe of the peaks of the Sierra Madre. Only a man like him would do such a mad thing — and remain a bandit too. His men grumbled a little and thought him slightly mad but they followed wherever he went. And the Conquistadores continued to raid and pillage.

In the mountain stronghold a son was born to the couple, and they named him Merton. Then Gomez, approaching middle-age, wanted to give up banditry. After that it was the old story once more of his flight, his poverty, and finally his betrayal by one of his own men and his sordid death at the hands of a blood-lusting vigilante mob.

His wife fled with her child. She reached the Mormon stronghold, Salt Lake City, and there she stayed. There, subsequently, a mistress among many, she died. Three months later, seventeen-year-old Merton ran away from his Mormon guardian, Abraham Scanlon, and worked his way south. All he had to remind him of his mother was a bronze medallion, a Mexican antique that his father had given her. Many months later, in San Antonio, he met Panhandle Jones. From his looks and the medallion he wore at his throat, the old man recognized him. The medallion had been hidden since, deep in the foot of Mert's right gun-holster, and his identity, that he was the son of the now fabulous 'hawk of the night' Gomez, was a great secret between Panhandle and himself. Even his best friend, the man who had first welcomed him at the Horse V ranch, Jack Sharp, did not know of it.

Mert rubbed himself with a rough towel until his body and his face glowed.

'Boilin' water here,' said Panhandle, and handed him a wicked-looking razor and a tablet of shaving-soap.

Mert found the mirror, soaped his face thickly and got to work. 'Got any scissors, ol' timer?' he said.

'Sure.' Somewhat mystified Panhandle handed them over. When Mert turned away from the mirror, wiping the soap from his face, the oldster gazed at him in astonishment. He had trimmed his moustache and beard but, apart from that, let them be: the clean-shaven Mert Scanlon was no more — a dark man with the beginnings of a handsome black beard had taken his place. Mert tugged at the long black locks of his hair. 'This won't do,' he said. He handed the scissors to Panhandle. 'Get tuh work, ol' timer.'

'Siddown,' said the old man. 'I've clipped hosses but I've had no practise at all with humans. I ain't promising it'll be purty.'

'Take plenty of it off that's all,' Mert told him.

'You'll suttinly look mighty different when I've finished with yuh,' Panhandle said. Then his voice sobered. 'Fresh clothes is what you want now,' he said. 'Somethin' to make yuh look less like a trouble-shootin' cowboy. Store-clothes maybe — an' a long black coat to hide them wicked-looking hawg-laigs. Pity you're so big — maybe I could've fixed you up with some of my old stuff, but I'll get yuh somep'n anyway while you're lyin' low.' Panhandle had forgotten his doubts now and he was entering into the deadly spirit of this masquerade. It was kind of exhilarating to be on the wrong side of the law again — if only in this small way.

★ ★ ★

As the candle clattered to the floor and went out, Jack Sharp did an unexpected thing. Instead of making a run for it, he dived at the bending Malone — or at least where he knew Malone was in the blackness. He hit the big man hard in the back. Malone grunted and spluttered as his face was buried in the damp straw.

Somebody shouted: 'Bronc! Where are yuh? What's happenin'?'

Jack reached for Malone's gun and found it. The big man tried to lift his head. Jack brought the gun-barrel down with savage force. Malone grunted once more and lay still. In the pitch-blackness, Jack crawled around against the wall of the cave. He dislodged a loose flint with a clatter that seemed deafening. He threw himself flat. A gun barked. The slug went wild, ricocheted from the hard rock and whined off in the blackness. The Double W man had pressed trigger out of sheer nervousness. Jack rose to his feet and began to run.

'He's makin' for the back end,' bawled a voice. 'Stop him! Get in front of him!'

Then Jack crashed into another running form. They rolled on the floor together. Jack rose, but other feet were before him, echoing in the tunnel. He was cut off.

He heard the man behind him rise,

and taking a chance, darted forward into the inky blackness of the tunnel. The Colt boomed so close to him that it blattered in his eardrums like a physical blow. He felt the breath of the slug, and cordite-laden smoke blew into his eyes and nostrils. He collided with the gunman and they went down in a tangled heap, rolling, fighting.

Jack heard somebody shout: 'Block the end of the passage.' Then he saw stars as a hard fist exploded in his face, bringing a gush of blood and searing pain to the wound Malone had made. Jack still gripped the gun as if it was part of him. He raised it and brought it down. He almost cried out with agony as it struck hard rock and the shock travelled to his shoulder, bringing sickening numbness for a moment. The other man was like an eel. Jack suddenly found himself grabbing mechanically at thin air.

A gun boomed again. The slug hit the floor somewhere to the right of Jack's head and ricocheted along the tunnel like an express-train. Jack rolled against the wall. These Double W boys certainly played for keeps. He heard one of them scuttling at the end of the tunnel, getting into position to cut him off. Then there was dead silence.

Jack began to rise slowly against the wall. He heard a faint movement and froze. This was a nerve-wracking cat-and-mouse game, and there was more than one cat. Jack knew that if he did not watch his step he had a good chance of being filled with slugs and buried down here in the blackness.

The silence now was like rushing water in his ears, coming from afar, muffled by a blanket that was black as pitch. He began to squirm along the wall again. He kicked at a stone and, as it clattered, dived desperately. Gunfire rolled like thunder again, echoing and reechoing. The cavern was lit spasmodically with flame. Sweat, cold as ice, beaded Jack's forehead as he rolled. Invisible fingers plucked at his sleeve, parted his hair. He rolled on his back and retaliated savagely, three shots in quick succession, then he rose and began to run. The man at the top of the passage opened up. Jack threw himself flat, knocking the breath from his body. He rolled and hugged the wall.

'Hold yuh fire, Olly,' shouted somebody behind him.

The man at the head of the tunnel replied: 'He's in the middle somewhere. He ain't got past me.'

Then from behind him again Jack heard a groan, but whether it was someone he had hit, or Malone coming round, he did not know. He rose again and began to move very slowly, painfully, along the wall.

A voice bawled: 'You'd better stand still, Sharp, an' give yuhself up. Yuh cain't get out.'

Jack did not reply. While the voice boomed in the tunnel he had gone a few more precious steps forward. He could almost sense the presence of the guard at the mouth of the tunnel, not very far in front of him now. If only he knew exactly where the fellow was. He would not hesitate to plug him — this guy had made it pretty clear that nothing was barred from now on. But he had only three bullets left — he could not afford to waste even one of them.

Then he heard the growling grumbling voice at the other end. Bronc Malone had come round. The voice rose to a bellow.

'Don't move, Sharp, or it'll be the wuss f'r yuh. Hold on, Olly, we're comin' down.'

Olly answered. 'He won't git past me.' Jack advanced quickly and fired. Olly cried out. Jack began to run. Boots thudded behind him. Another gun boomed and he felt a searing pain like a red-hot sword in his side. It knocked him flat on his face. As he struggled to rise, the thudding footsteps were coming nearer. He managed to get to his feet and ran on. Wave after wave of nausea was driving him back from his objective. He stumbled and fell again.

Then a heavy body crashed on top of him. 'Got him,' a voice bawled triumphantly.

Dazed and beaten he was hauled to his feet and dragged back along the passage to the cavern. One of the men lit the candle once more. Its flickering light threw their black grotesque shadows on the smooth wall and, fantastically elongated, on the craggy ceiling. A man limped into the circle of light.

'Where did he get yuh, Olly?' said Malone.

'Just a graze in the leg,' said the guard.

Jack Sharp raised himself out of his pain and sickness. 'Pity,' he said. 'I meant tuh kill yuh.'

Bronc Malone's face seemed to glow devilishly in the half-light. He said: 'You've had a long run, Sharp. We're gonna finish you off right now.'

Jack saw the gun in his hand flash as it was raised and he instinctively ducked. The gun-barrel crashed on his shoulder and he sagged at the knees. Through a haze of pain, fighting to rise again, he saw Malone wheel. Olly, beside him, turning too, raising his gun, but the shot did not come from either of them and it was Olly who crumpled while Malone, with a curse, threw himself to one side.

'Back up,' snarled a familiar voice. 'Back up.'

The Double W men backed away, leaving a clear circle of light around the swaying Jack. It spread to the step where stood two men. Steel glittered in their hands. Their faces were shrouded in shadow but Jack had no difficulty in recognizing them. They were his pards of the afternoon — oh, so long ago — Arizona and Gyp.

'Think you can manage tuh get their guns, Jack?' said Arizona.

'You betcha,' said the cowboy. He straightened up miraculously and went around relieving the Double W men of their hardware. The luckless Olly lay on his back, the candlelight gleaming horribly on the whites of his staring, sightless eyes.

Jack piled the guns on the straw in the corner of the cave. Arizona and Gyp descended the steps.

Jack said: 'I'll go up in front if yuh like an' wait for 'em tuh come up.' He found his own two guns among the pile and slid them into their greased holsters. He felt a whole lot better now.

'All right,' said Arizona. Jack passed them, ascended the steps, and went through the wide-open trap into the cabin. He leaned against the huge packing case and took out his guns once more.

He could see better up here, the darkness was not so absolute. He levelled the guns at the black hole in the floor and waited.

He heard Arizona yell: 'Git movin', an' no funny business. All right — we'll send fer him later.' And that last sentence was Olly's epitaph.

The first head appeared above the hole and Jack recognized Malone.

'Take it easy, Bronc,' he said. 'Get over towards the door. An' remember, I'd willingly kill yuh . . . There — that'll do!'

One by one the men came into the cabin, Arizona and Gyp in the rear. Then the three Horse V waddies shepherded the disarmed men out into the open.

'What shall we do with 'em?' said Arizona.

'A nice long limb oughta do it,' said Gyp with ghoulish humour.

It was Jack who was left to make the final decision. He knew he was in a kind of ticklish position himself. He said: 'I guess all we kin do right now is turn 'em loose. But we'll make 'em walk back to the Double W. Stampede their hosses.'

'It goes against the grain,' said Arizona. 'But wal . . . ' He couldn't think of anything else.

Gyp delightedly began to run the Double W horses off. Then the three Horse V men mounted.

Before he rode away, Jack Sharp looked down at Bronc Malone and said:

'I'll see you again.'

The big waddy knew what he meant. 'I'll be waitin',' he replied. Jack Sharp tumbled from his horse as they entered the Horse V stables. He had a slug between his ribs.

6

'Don't Let It Throw Yuh'

The rest of the night was very hazy for the freckle-faced ranny. He was vaguely aware of the rough, but kindly ministrations of the Old Man; a wave of blinding pain as the slug was extracted; of being wound like a mummy in bandages. The bunk in which he lay seemed unusually soft: he realized later that it was a spare bed in the ranch house.

By morning he was sitting-up and taking notice. Doc Larson had been fetched from town. He said Jack had nothing to worry about; the fever had abated and a few days in bed would put him right.

Then the Old Man came in again; with him were Arizona and Gyp.

Old Hank said: 'I saw yuh leavin' the

ranch last night. I had an idea yuh might be goin' tuh see that pesky pard o' yourn. I didn't want to see yuh get in no trouble so I sent these boys after yuh.'

'Lucky f'r me yuh did. They suttinly saved my bacon.' Jack swivelled his head. 'I ain't had a chance tuh thank you boys properly before. I'm suttinly obliged — that's the second time too . . . '

'Fergit it, Jack,' said Arizona.

'Yeah,' said Gyp. 'Allus glad to have a crack at that Malone an' his buzzards.'

'You wuz lucky shore 'nough though,' said Arizona. 'We lost yuh once. Then we figured yuh must've gone intuh the ol' line hut. We wuz nearly there when we heard other hosses. Then they stopped. Any way we pushed on as quietly as possible an' reached the ol' hut. We found the hosses — an' the one on its lonesome was yours. We hid our own cayusses an' went forward on foot . . . '

'Wobbled more like,' grinned little

Gyp. 'I'd got the heebie-jeebies right down to muh ankles.'

Then the redhead continued: 'Wal — we got inside the hut, but there was nobody there. Not knowin' about the secret trap, o' course, we was plumb throwed an' hogtied — we didn't know which way tuh turn. Then I thought I heard voices — a sort of mumblin' right in the air . . . '

'I said it wuz thunder,' said Gyp. 'But he kept saying it wuz voices. We searched the hut an' couldn't find anythin'. By that time I could heah the mumblin' as well. Made muh knees knock I might tell yuh . . . '

His redheaded pardner grinned. 'Gyp thought it wuz spooks,' he said. 'But we figured it must be the people we wuz lookin' for. But where were they? I said the mumblin' seemed to come from somewhere round the back o' the hut so we went outside and round the back. Then we heard the shots — kinda muffled as if they came from under the ground. We dashed back into the hut —

the shooting wuz plainer in there. We managed to trace the sound, an' after grubbin' around a mite an' burnin' our fingers with matches we found the trap. You know what happened after that.'

'Yeah,' said Jack. 'An' Olly moved a mite too quickly. You had tuh plug him. If yuh hadn't there'd've bin a real murder jamboree down thet cellar.'

'We're goin' into town right now to report everythin' tuh the sheriff,' said the Old Man. 'One thing I wanta know fust: what happened to Mert Scanlon?'

'He'd gone before I got there,' said Jack. 'He left a note in the cavern. I think it's in my vest pocket. Have a look, boss, will yuh?'

Hank Bulger found the crumpled piece of paper and smoothed it out. He read it aloud. Then he said: 'This don't tell anybody much, does it. This all you know, Jack?'

'Yes, all! I know no more than anybody else now.'

'I'll haveta give this tuh the sheriff,' said the Old Man. 'Jest tuh be on the level — but I guess it won't tell him nothin'.' His gimlet grey eyes bored into the man in bed. 'We'll tell him yuh rode to the line-hut thinking maybe Mert 'ud be hidin' there — as yuh both knew o' the secret passage. 'Pears like Mert figured you might so he left a note jest in case. We won't tell the sheriff you knew Mert wuz there all along. That's what he'll figure but I guess it cain't do no harm 'less he kin prove it.'

'That note's kind of incriminatin',' said Jack.

The Old Man sighed and took the crumpled paper from his pocket. He fumbled again and struck a match on his heel. He applied the flame to the corner of the paper. They watched it flame, in silence, until it was fine ash on the rush carpet. The Old Man said: 'I ain't doin' this f'r Mert Scanlon, Jack, I'm doin' it f'r you.'

'Thanks, boss,' said the cowboy softly.

His freckled face was marred by a long strip of plaster that ran from his temple to the corner of his mouth. It seemed that even when the wound was healed he would be marked for life. The insult was the worst of it: to be pistol-whipped was a degradation.

He said: 'I guess I'm causin' yuh a peck o' trouble, boss. But — but yuh know, don't yuh? — I gotta get that Malone now.'

'Yeah, I know, son,' the Old Man's voice was almost kindly. 'But we'll talk about thet later . . . Right now we gotta put Arizona right about that Olly *hombre* he shot.'

'It wuz plain self-defence,' said Jack.

'Yeah,' said Arizona. 'But I bet the Double W boys are in town right now tryin' tuh make it out murder.'

Subsequent events proved him correct. A gun-battle in town between the Double W and Horse V men later that morning was nipped in the bud by the sheriff and a bunch of deputies he had recently sworn-in. The sheriff returned to the Horse V with old Hank and the boys and came in to interview Jack. He got no change out of the freckle-faced cowboy, whose own condition was proof that the mêlée in the secret passage in which Olly had been killed, had not all been one-sided.

'It wuz a cunning scheme on Malone's part,' Jack told him. 'If Arizona and Gyp hadn't turned up I'd've bin plugged out of hand and left down in that passage tuh rot. The Double W boys would've kept quiet about the passage and everybody would've thought I'd hightailed with Mert Scanlon.'

'If you know where Scanlon is you'd better tell me,' said Sheriff Blackson. ''Cos we're sure tuh get him sooner or later.'

'I don't know where he is,' said Jack.

Blackson did not press the case. Jack had the idea he was hanging fire.

He made one significant remark before he left. 'If you an' Bronc Malone've gotta tangle I hope you blow each other's haids off.' His long sour face scowled. Then the door closed on it.

Jack leaned back on the pillows. Yeah, he meant to tangle with Malone all right. Just as soon as was able. He reached the makings from his little bedside table and began to roll himself a cigarette, wincing a little as the movements sent pain shooting through his wounded side. He dragged deeply at the soothing weed and began to think things over . . . His volatile pard — his right-hand man for so many years — was gone. Jack knew not where. Mert was an outcast now, a hunted killer. Things had changed so very quickly — and yet Jack could not get the thought out of his mind of the inevitability of it all — as if Mert was made for the owlhoot and he himself was being dragged irrevocably after him. The gun-battle with Malone would maybe be the first step but he had no thoughts of avoiding it. Maybe it was the point where everything would be decided one way or another . . . He wondered where Mert was now.

His speculations were interrupted by sharp footsteps in the passage, then someone rapped the door. He said: 'Come in.' The door opened and Judy Hodgeson entered.

She was clad in riding-clothes. A Mexican style black vest, embroidered with silver braid, over a light brown shirtwaist. Her narrow gunbelt was chased in silver, as was the holster that held a small pearl-handled automatic. Her riding-slacks were dark-brown, her riding-boots, with ornamental tops, also in silver — as were the small blunt spurs at her heels. She removed her wide-brimmed, black sombrero as she entered the room, and with an unconscious gesture, shook free the long blonde waves of her hair, her blue eyes sparkled. She was no belle of the barbecue now, but a girl of the open spaces, bringing the sun, the travelling breeze, the smell of the sagebrush into the little room.

Jack stubbed out his cigarette and

drew himself up. He felt suddenly embarrassed: an old crock skulking in bed before such young, healthy loveliness.

'Morning, Jack,' she said.

Her voice was like the musical tinkle of water over sun-warmed stones. Maybe Jack's unwonted helplessness and wounds had made him lame-brained and fanciful but that's how it sounded to him.

'Mornin', Judy,' he said huskily. 'How are you feeling?'

'Fine.'

She sat in the cane-bottomed armchair beside the bed. His unwonted awkwardness left him. A youthful stripling himself when he joined the Horse V he had seen the girl from the neighbouring Pinwheel jump from a gangling, coltish adolescent to a beautiful young woman with all the natural coquetry of her sex. It was a sex he didn't know much about and had never had a lot to do with — maybe that's why Judy and he had always been good pals, allied to the fact that her swain, Mert, was his best friend. Mert was the more handsome, he had always been the best dancer, the best hand with the girls. And Jack had been content to let it be that way. He was a man's man, a cowhand, a gambler, a fast-gun if need be. Many said he was the finest in the territory. He liked disciplined action; only the fact that he liked his job and his pards on the Horse V so much had prevented him from taking up a lawman's job years ago. Fat chance he'd got now anyway.

He and the girl talked cheerful commonplaces, both of them stifling their forebodings, and Mert Scanlon's name was not mentioned at all. Finally the girl excused herself and rose.

'Don't let it throw yuh, pard,' she said boyishly. 'You'll be up an' around in no time.'

She flipped her hand to him and went. He heard her high heeled riding-boots clack-clack along the passage and down the stairs, then cross the veranda till they faded away in the yard. A few moments later he heard her horse galloping away. In his mind there were two Judys. One, the dolled-up, flirty, rather empty-headed belle of the barbecue with all the feminine fripperies and wiles that unnerved and irritated him; and the other, the one he had just seen; the free-and-easy, comradely girl of the plains — the one he liked and admired.

He lay back on his pillows and his mind built up visions of her. Then he suddenly shook his sandy head vigorously. What the hell was the matter with him? Was he completely haywire? Had his rough handling at the hands of the Double W men addled his brain? A salty son-of-a-gun like him didn't want no truck with women. Particularly one who was, as far as he was concerned, his best friend's girl.

★　★　★

It was late at night when the horseman rode into the shadows of Panhandle Jones's stables and the oldtimer came out to meet him. He peered short-sightedly at the newcomer. Even in San Antonio such late arrivals were pretty rare.

'Howdy,' he said.

As he went closer and the stranger began to dismount, something about the man's stalwart bearing seemed very familiar to Panhandle. Then when a voice said: 'Hullo, ol'timer,' he was sure of the man's identity.

'Lemmy!' he said. 'I thought you wuz out on an assignment.'

'I was,' said Lemmy Buxton, Texas Ranger. 'I ain't supposed to be here. Nobody knows I've come back yet 'cept you. I wound the job up faster than I figured. The *hombre* I wuz after fell down a cliff face an' broke his neck. I came right back. Thought me an' you could have a pow-wow.'

'Yeah, sure, Lemmy,' said the old man. 'I'll see to yuh hoss. Go intuh the kitchen if yuh like.'

'I'll stay here an' talk to yuh,' said the Ranger.

He paused, then he said: 'You know me, Panhandle, I don't flap my jaw f'r nothin'. What I gotta say may be important — it may not. Hear me out an' tell me what you think, what yuh know — if yuh kin tell me anythin' at all.'

'Sure, Lemmy,' said Panhandle. His face hidden in the gloom, he busied himself with the horse.

Lemmy said: 'In Laredo I met Whitey Porter.'

'Whitey, the gambler? I thought he wuz still in San Antonio.'

'No, it seems he left not so long after me . . . We got tuh talking about the Johnson killin' — as yuh know, its the big news o' the moment — an' Whitey said a mighty funny thing.' Lemmy paused again.

Panhandle stood erect, looking, waiting. Lemmy lit a cigarette and took a couple of deep pulls.

'What was this mighty funny thing Whitey said, Lemmy?' asked Panhandle.

'Wa-al — it seems Whitey thought he saw Mert Scanlon in San Antonio jest 'fore he left.'

'So,' said Panhandle.

'He couldn't be sure mind you . . . This fellow who looked like Scanlon came ridin' into San Antonio that night jest 'fore Whitey left. He looked as if he'd bin ridin' long an' hard an' he badly needed a shave — that's why Whitey wasn't sure it was Scanlon, not knowin' the feller real well-like either. But he kept his eyes on him an' he saw him come here . . . '

'Here?'

'Yeah, here — in these stables. An' Whitey didn't see him come out agin thet night tho' o'course he didn't stop too late. The law had told him to get out o' San Antonio an' he had to git before mornin'. Little matter o' too many cold decks an' double-shuffles.' Lemmy paused. Then he said: 'I got tuh thinkin'. I remembered you knew Mert Scanlon well. He useter come here quite a lot, time back . . . It's feasible that bein' on the run, he'd come to his ol' pard again. Did he come here that night, Panhandle? An' where is he now?'

'One question at a time,' said the old man. 'No, Mert Scanlon ain't bin here. An' I don't know' where he is now.' Some of the old spirit of hate — hate of the law, came back and his voice rose. 'An if I did know where he wuz I wouldn't tell a snooping bounty-hunter like you who don't trust his own friends.' He stopped, his older caution returning: he could have bitten his tongue out.

Lemmy Buxton spoke again and his voice was cold as ice. 'I figure I'd like to look your place over, Panhandle.'

The old man shrugged in the darkness. 'Suit yourself. Yuh know your way around.'

The ranger made for the kitchen. He pushed open the door and went in.

131

Something crackled above Panhandle's head. Then a tall figure dropped catfooted beside him, and sped towards the door.

'Take it easy, son,' whispered Panhandle as he followed.

The ranger whirled as the door opened. His hand dropped towards the guns low-slung on his thighs. Then they stopped at the menace of the Colts in the tall, bearded man's hands; the killer-light in his dark eyes.

'So you were here all the time, Scanlon?'

'Yeah. Take his guns, Panhandle.'

The old man hesitated a fraction between the two. Both of them, despite his outburst at the ranger a few moments ago, were still his friends.

Then he crossed the room. 'Got tuh do this, Lemmy,' he said, and took the guns.

'Give 'em tuh me, Panhandle,' said Mert.

The old man handed them over and the tall man tucked them both into his belt. 'Saddle up my hoss,' he said. The old man shuffled away into the stable.

'What are yuh goin tuh do, Scanlon?' said Lemmy.

'You'll see.'

'We'll get yuh in the finish yuh know. We allus do.'

'Save it,' said Mert. He jerked one gun meaningly. 'Come on. Git goin'.' He moved aside to let the ranger pass him. He shepherded him through the door into the stables.

'Ready, Panhandle?' he said.

'Yeah — ready!'

'Git on your nag, ranger.'

The ranger mounted and moved out of the stall.

'That'll do.' Mert mounted his own horse. 'All right. Git goin' — easy. An' remember I've got a gun on your back an' won't hesitate tuh shoot.'

'I ain't aimin' tuh commit suicide,' said Lemmy.

As the two horsemen moved out of the stables, Panhandle said: 'Don't treat him too rough, Mert. He's still a friend of mine.'

'I'll jest take him out an' lose him,' said Mert. '*Adios, amigo.*'

'*Adios.*'

His old shoulders bent, the old man went back into the gloom. He heard the soft hoof-thuds fade away in the distance.

7

'That's Len Kane'

The stagecoach from San Antonio pulled up with a screeching and a clattering outside its usual post in San Martini, the Golden Pesos Saloon. Here it always lingered awhile to feed and refresh men and beasts, and sometimes — but very rarely — to drop passengers before it careered on to Laredo. This particular morning the eyes of the loungers almost popped out of their heads as the stage began to disgorge passengers like coloured ribbons out of the mouth of a conjuror. First, a dapper little man, incongruous in a black cutaway and pipe-stem pinstripes. Then a huge man with a bowler hat on his bullet head, rough tweeds on his bulging body and outsize high-boots on his lower extremities.

This bruiser turned to give his arm to a thin, yellow-featured oldster in rusty black who swept the small crowd with cold, hard, fish-like eyes. Lastly came a Westerner with professional gunman written all over him: hawk-like features, eyes like chips of ice, mouth like a thin tight gash. Black-handled Colts, very low in their holsters, were tied to his bulging thighs by whangstrings.

One of the loungers recognized him and whispered: 'That's Len Kane.'

A cold shiver seemed to pass through the group. US Marshal Len Kane, ruthless manhunter and gunman par excellence, was bad news for any town.

Kane stormed on the boardwalk, and speaking to nobody in particular said: 'Where can I find the sheriff?' His voice carried a note of authority.

One of the loungers said: 'I guess he's in his office. Jest down the street a piece.' He pointed. 'Yuh cain't miss it.'

As Kane said 'Thanks,' a man jumped from the box beside the driver and joined the marshal. He was younger, leaner. His hair was long and yellow and he looked as mean as a lobo wolf.

'C'mon, Flash,' said Kane. The two men went down the street. The coach guard was handing down boxes and suitcases, a seemingly endless stream of them to the bruiser fellow, who handled them as if they were feather pillows. The dapper little man bustled through the ranks of the loungers and into Tubby La Rue's Golden Pesos. The lean oldster raked the gawping faces with his fish-like eyes and his bloodless lips curled. Then he went and sat on the end of the bench in the shade of the porch. The town wit was sitting on the other end but he quickly moved. He said the old Easterner made him feel melancholy.

In the saloon, the dapper little man accosted Tubby La Rue. 'Where can I get a conveyance?' he rapped.

The fat saloonkeeper blinked his little eyes in sleepy surprise at such bombast and said: 'Plenty o' hosses in the stables.'

'Horses?' echoed the little man. His voice got shrill. 'Horses did you say? I want a carriage of some kind, man, to take myself and Mr Emanuel Johnson and his — er — man to the Double W Ranch.'

Tubby's eyes opened just a little wider. 'Colly Johnson's pa?' he said.

'Who else? And he isn't used to being kept waiting.'

'So,' said Tubby. He yawned in the little pipsqueak's face. 'Wal, mebbe one o' the livery-stable people kin find you somethin'. I run a saloon — now, ef'n you'd like a drink.'

The little man had seemed on the verge of an explosion but the magic word drink quietened him down.

'Well,' he said. 'Ahem.' He turned and scuttled away.

When he returned he had Emmanuel Johnson with him. They sat at a table in a shady corner and the little man who, after some hesitation, introduced

138

himself to Tubby as Hiram Bloomfield, Mr Johnson's legal adviser, came to the bar and ordered two soft drinks.

He whispered: 'This is the first time Mr Johnson has been in a saloon for a good many years. He's a leader of the anti-alcohol campaign.'

Meanwhile, the Chicago millionaire sat in his corner like a predatory shadow and weighed up everything and everybody. These people had reviled his son, had murdered him. They would rue the day Emmanuel Johnson arrived at their stinking God-forsaken little town.

Presently the big man came into the saloon and went over to the table in the corner. He stood there respectfully, like a huge, misshapen dummy until his master looked up and said:

'Yes, Pilson?'

'I've found a horse an' trap, sir,' said Pilson. 'It's ready outside. An' a man to drive it, sir.'

'Very well, Pilson.' Emmanuel rose and placed a yellow claw on the bruiser's thick arm. The ill-assorted trio passed out of the saloon.

Meanwhile, in the office down the street, Len Kane was preaching to sour-faced Sheriff Blackson.

'So this Scanlon *hombre* jest vanished like the ground swallowed him, huh? An' you nearly had him once. Fine deputies you must have tuh get themselves shot like that. Sump'ns gotta be done mighty quick I'll tell yuh — that's why I've been sent here by the special request o' Johnson Senior; he's out for blood believe me. That young skunk who got himself shot was the apple of his eye. They say the ol' man bawled at the great funeral they had after the body was taken there. Bawled I tell yuh — him! You ain't seen him. Wait till yuh do. He's here — here, right now — an' he means to take this place apart. Somebody's gotta pay — an' pay mighty quick.'

The marshal stopped talking. His abysmal eyes raked the sheriff. This sour-faced jasper was a cool customer anyway. He didn't seem to have turned a hair.

The marshal turned and took a cigarette from his yellow-haired deputy, Flash Kramar. They lit up. Neither of them offered one to the sheriff. He took a packet of long, Mexican cheroots from his desk-drawer and lit one for himself. Although he looked calm enough, his quick movements betrayed his nervousness. Kane turned on him again.

'All right,' he said. 'Let's have it all. Right from the beginning.

The sheriff began to talk in his slightly querulous voice. He resented this other lawman, but he knew his reputation and had more sense than to voice his thoughts. US Marshal Kane could break him — in more ways than one.

When the sheriff had concluded his narrative, Kane said:

'I aim tuh start at the bottom again. First tuh see the girl an' that trouble-shootin' pardner o' Scanlan's. It seems tuh me either — or both — o' them two should know where he's hidin' out. Every lawman in the state is looking f'r him. Nobody's seen him or heard of him. It ain't natural. The logical conclusion is that he's bein' hidden by friends . . . Thet gel fer instance: I guess she ain't told everythin'. It wuz for her thet Scanlon shot Johnson. Seems to me she wuz playing both ends against the middle. Scanlon's sweet on her all right. She's probably sweet on him too. She stuck up for him afterwards didn't she? Yeah, I guess she'll maybe know where he is.'

'I have her watched everywhere she goes,' said the sheriff. 'She only goes ridin' now an' then. Nowhere special. I don't think she knows anythin'. She jest happened tuh get herself in an unfortunate position that's all. She's a nice kid.' He was defending Judy now out of pure cussedness.

'They allus are nice kids,' drawled Flash Kramar.

Those were the first words he had

spoken since he entered the office. They were characteristic of his brutality and cynicism.

'We want a couple of good hosses,' said Kane.

'I can get 'em for yuh,' said the sheriff and rose. They followed him into the street. 'After we've had some chow an' a clean-up we'll do some ridin' with yuh, sheriff,' said Kane.

'Just as you say, marshal,' said Blackson.

As the three men strode down the street, the horse and trap bearing Emmanuel and his two minions was just beginning to move. The marshal cuffed his hat. Emmanuel inclined his head slightly. His mouth was a stretched gash as the trap jolted away.

'Thet's ol' Johnson I guess,' said Blackson.

'Yeah,' said the marshal.

The sour-faced sheriff's silence was more eloquent than words.

The marshal and his deputy hired horses from the Cameo Stables. They had brought their riding tackle with them. They had a meal in the nearby Joe-Bow Eating Place. Stifling his reluctance, the sheriff joined them.

'Hadn't I better git a few men together?' he said.

'We don't need any men,' said Kane curtly.

A little later the three men left San Martini and set off across the mesa. The loungers' eyes came out on sticks to watch them until they were a dust puff in the distance. Speculation hummed like a hive of worried hornets. This day, San Martini had certainly got itself a place in the sun. A sun that was likely to blister the hide right off'n it.

Mrs Hodgeson received the law at the Pinwheel. Both her husband and daughter were out riding. The marshal could ask her anything he wanted to know. Even Len Kane found himself a little nonplussed by the bright, forthright manner of this spare woman. He was saved from embarrassment by the sudden arrival of Nat and Judy. The

Marshal weighed-up the man: a homesteader who had carved a place for himself; taciturn, pugnacious, stubborn. He had handled his sort before. The girl was harder to classify. She was certainly a mighty pretty little filly. She looked straight, too: but you never could tell. Kane did not profess to know a lot about the fairer sex. He could not understand anybody fighting over 'em. And killing . . . He wondered what Flash, a deadly lady's-man, thought about the filly.

The sheriff introduced him. Nat Hodgeson's lean face hardened when he heard the name.

'I'd like to ask your daughter some questions, Mr Hodgeson,' said Kane. The rancher was not fooled by the commonplace tones. He knew the marshal's deadly reputation. But Judy had nothing to fear from such as he. He looked interrogatively at the girl.

Judy looked squarely at the gunman. 'What do you want to know?'

Kane began his catechism. The girl's

answers were quiet and to the point. He didn't get any place at all. She was making him look kind of small before the sheriff and he did not like it. His gall began to show.

Hodgeson moved up beside his daughter. 'She don't know anythin', marshal,' he said. 'You ought to be able to see that.'

'Keep out of it, pop,' said slit-eyed Flash Kramar who, up till then, had been ogling the girl. His thumbs were hooked in his belt close to the walnut-butts of his guns. There was tension in the air.

'Of course she doesn't know anything,' said a calm feminine voice. 'The marshal knows that. He's no fool.'

The tension was dispelled. It was as if a clot of hot air had been blown away by a cool breeze.

Almost as a matter of form, Kane said: 'So you cain't give us any idea where Scanlon might be, Miss Hodgeson? No thought, no hint?'

'Not a thing, marshal.'

'All right.' The marshal wheeled his horse.

Mother, father and daughter watched the trio ride away.

Nat Hodgeson said: 'There go two dangerous *hombres*.' Then he echoed all their thoughts. 'I hope Jack Sharp don't go an' tangle with 'em.'

At the same time, Kane was saying: 'Folks like that wouldn't talk even if they knew anythin'. That's what you're up against in these hick territories. The folks stick together closer than clams. They'd shield a maniac if he wuz a neighbour o' theirs.'

'Mebbe you're kind of prejudiced,' said Flash with a thin lopsided smile that did not reach his eyes.

'Mebbe we'll get on better with this salty hellion at the other show,' said Kane.

Sheriff Blackson was silent. He was wondering whether Jack Sharp, the fastest gun in the territory, could haze these two professionals if need be.

That night was black; the sky was a

hot, prickly blanket pressing on the heads of any wanderers luckless enough to be out beneath it. San Antonio slept uncomfortably. A whistle piped miserably as the night-train of the Southern Pacific moved out of the deserted siding. The two horsemen who rode across the mesa, strung out one behind the other like a pair of puppies, seemed the only living things on an earth that the elements were trying to stifle.

The man in front turned his head and said: 'Where we making for?'

The other said: 'You'll find out. Keep movin'.'

A distant roll of thunder followed his words like an ominous warning.

'Better get near shelter anyway,' called the first man. 'We don't want to get wet.'

'You ain't got nothin' to worry about,' said the man behind. 'Quit gabbin'.'

Again that ominous rolling, like a question-mark after his words, and sounding louder this time. Away in the

East somewhere the sky was lightened suddenly by a blur of lightning.

The man in front started to turn his horse.

'This fool game's gone far enough,' he yelled. 'What air you aimin' tuh do. Do it an' get it over with.'

'Get back,' said the other. 'I shouldn't like tuh plug yuh right now. But I ain't playing no games. Get on a mite faster — an' remember: I'm right behind yuh.'

The first man turned his horse's head once more and pressed forward at a faster pace. The first large drop of rain plummeted from the black sky and the thunder rolled along overhead.

Lightning flashed nearer, etching the black figures of the two horsemen in their strange cavalcade. The foremost horse snorted in fright and reared a little. Its rider gentled it with a hand on its glossy neck. The man behind jerked erect in the saddle. The lightning flashed on the blue steel of the gun in his hand.

The rain fell with a sudden rush. The man behind saw the other like a shifting mirage through a shimmering green screen. He urged his horse forward.

Both horses were moving faster now, with exhilaration rather than fear, as the lowering skies lightened and the rain brought coolness. The man behind caught up and kept close behind his quarry. He shouted something. It sounded like 'No funny business!' but the chuckling rain juggled with the words and tossed them away.

Lightning split the sky once more. The foremost horse reared, and as its front hoofs came down again, stretched out in a loping gallop. Its rider yippeed shrilly, lying over its neck. The man gentled his plunging mount and yelled, then he too set his horse at a breakneck gallop.

The long wet grass swished at the beasts' legs, the rain slashed at horses and riders as they bored through it. The lightning flashed fitfully, lighting up the figures in this nightmare race. They were like phantoms from another sphere battling for supremacy on this rolling plateau, this deserted land beneath the sky.

The horses' hoofs began to thud on ground composed of a mixture of sand and rock. Then the first horse reared suddenly on a lip of rock, on the edge of a dark chasm. Down below, water rushed and blustered. The rider dismounted.

The second man dismounted a few yards away. His hands were tucked into his sides, sheltered steel gleamed dully in the wet half-light. The skies were broken now, drifting, spiralling clouds. The rain had spent out its passion and was drumming with a steady monotony. The man shouted: 'Misjudged a little, didn't yuh? I thought you knew your territory better'n that. That's the Colorado.' He began to come nearer.

The man at the edge of the gash said: 'Wal, it wuz a good race while it lasted. Now what?' He went nearer to the edge, peering into the murk; here and there, far below, water shone like crystals.

The man at the back said: 'Jump over.'

The other turned away from the edge and took a few steps.

'Go on. Jump.'

'An' what if I don't?' He still advanced slowly.

'That way I'm givin' yuh a fifty-fifty chance . . . Keep your distance, man, or I'll shoot.' The gunman's eyes glared in the darkness.

'Shoot an' be damned to yuh.' The other man crouched a little, still coming on.

'Turn around you fool. You gotta better chance the other way.'

This time the advancing man did not speak. The gunman's teeth bared whitely. He seemed to be trembling with rage in the shimmering rain.

'You're askin' for it.' He spread his legs. The gun in his hand poked out a little from cover then went back again.

He scraped one foot along a little way

in front of the other. The two men watched each other like gladiators. One, crouching a little, still moving. The other erect, his eyes glaring as if the passion inside him was trying to break through them into flame. Then the second man rushed.

The other levelled his gun. The hammer clicked dully on a damp cartridge. Then he sidestepped, sliding the gun into its holster, meeting the other's rush with a broad shoulder.

'If that's the way you want it,' he said. His voice was like the hiss of an angry snake.

They grappled, swaying in the rain. They broke and parted then came on again, throwing blows. They were like moving phantoms in a wet wilderness — warring for supremacy. Two tried, well-matched gladiators, hardly distinguishable, one from the other, in the driving rain which chuckled at their folly while goading them on. They were like dripping abysmal beasts, grunting now, with the thud of hard fists, striking flesh.

One of them went down, the other on top of him. They rolled, a threshing mass of arms and legs. They rose, flailing at each other. One of them was spreadeagled again by a terrific blow. The other dived at him. Locked together they rolled to the lip of the dark chasm.

8

'What Can the Law Do?'

Marshal Len Kane's interview with Jack Sharp was more than a little one-sided. The cowboy reclined in an armchair on the porch of the ranch house. It was his first day out of bed and the doc had told him to take it easy. Like he told the three lawmen, 'He was jest restin'-up a mite, but 'ud be as right as rain in a couple o' days.' He did not deign to rise.

He answered the marshal's questions blandly. 'Right now,' he said, 'he felt kinda tuckered out an' wasn't worryin' his little haid about nothin'. He didn't know where Mert Scanlon was an' he was doin' no figurin' about it a'tall.'

Kane knew he was being joshed; knew that his reputation meant nothing to this freckle-faced ranny. He'd like to blast him right out of that chair. However, he controlled his voice admirably when, at the end of the conversation, he said:

'From now on I'm the law in this territory, Mr Sharp, an' I aim tuh do things my way. I guess you people here don't cotton on tuh such changes.'

'Mebbe not.'

'Mebbe you'll be leavin' the territory when you're fit enough?'

The cowboy with the strip of sticking plaster down one cheek, did not turn a hair. He said: 'Yeah, I had thought about ridin' — when I've seen to one or two little chores that've got to be done.'

He meant what he said. He had been figuring that way of late. As he watched the three lawmen ride away, his assumed lethargy dropped from him like a cloak; his brain worked busily . . .

But to no purpose. He was hogtied again. He saw another rider approaching the ranch house. He was not surprised to recognize Judy Hodgeson. She came to see him about this time every day, and he had to admit he looked forward to her visits with eagerness. With a sudden flash of blinding clarity he decided that maybe she was the reason his thoughts had turned to leaving. He, who was frightened of no man, scared stiff of a chit of a girl — his best friend's girl to boot.

He sighed a little and rose to meet her.

'Be careful of that side, Jack,' she called. 'Sit down.'

Obediently he seated himself once more. Trim and cool she mounted the steps, drew another chair up beside him and sat down. They uttered the usual commonplaces, chaffing each other a little almost like two men rather than a man and a girl. As usual, she stayed about ten minutes, then, with a comradely flip of her hand, went on her way.

Jack leaned back in his chair, smoking, and wrestled with his thoughts once more. It seemed like he,

the cautious level-headed fighting man,
was rolling on a barrel.

★   ★   ★

Events moved pretty swiftly in the next
few days. Marshal Kane and his deputy,
Flash Kragar, moved into quarters in
town and went out riding and asking
questions continually. Nobody knew
anything, but they could not convince
the marshal of that fact. He was sure
that a good many people knew of the
whereabouts of the vanished killer,
Mert Scanlon. Somebody might even
be hiding him right here in the
territory. Flash had a run-in with a
drunken cowboy who resented his
arrogance. The deputy demonstrated
his skill with a smoke-pole by shooting
two of the luckless waddy's fingers off
before they had even touched the gun
they reached for.

But even this incident was of
secondary importance to the behaviour
of Emmanuel Johnson, who had already

begun to show the cloven hoof. Don George Gabazo felt the back-lash of it first.

The creek at which his cattle drank ran through a corner of Double W land. The Mexican spread had no water of its own, as the river that bounded its other side was unfit for that purpose. The Don had always had access to the little creek although it did not run through his land. It slashed the territory of the Double W, the Pinwheel and the Horse V. The water-rights legally belonged equally to these three spreads but no one, not even the arrogant younger Johnson, had begrudged the old Mexican his use of the creek. This was the only stretch of territory Colly Johnson had not dared fence, but his father had no such timidity or scruples. A few days after his arrival, he had a gang of men stringing barbed-wire between the creek and Don George's land.

Thirsty cattle coming down to drink were driven back by rifle fire, leaving behind a few of their number; still heaps in the long grass. Three *vaqueros* coming to investigate were driven back too, and rode post-haste back to the hacienda with the news. The hot-headed young Pedro wanted to take a force of men out pronto and meet this violation of unwritten Western law with its proper medicine — hot lead. But his father, the old Don, with the wisdom of age, thought not. Perhaps that was just what Johnson wanted them to do.

By sundown, the fast-working mob of Double W men had finished their task, but they left guards with the newest high-powered rifles to guard the stretch of fence and the creek. These men, who expected trouble and were ready for it, were surprised by the quietness of the night, broken only by occasional nocturnal visits to the fence by thirsty steers.

Don George had decided that his herd, which had plenty of lush grass, would not come to much harm through abstaining from fresh water for a day. Tomorrow he would go to the law at

San Martini and have things put to rights. Pedro had better come with him. The ranch would be left in charge of the ramrod, Jules Manton, who was older and wiser, and never did anything drastic without orders.

The next morning the Gabazos, father and son, drove their buckboard to San Martini and saw the sheriff. He, with a scowl, washed his hands of the matter — 'seemed like right now he was jest nobody in this territory' — and referred them to Marshal Len Kane. They found the marshal in an office he had fixed himself up in the lower front room of the lodging-house where he and his deputy had rooms.

The hawk-faced lawman, with the yellow-haired Flash at his side, listened to the complaint of the old Mexican. Kane's poker-face gave nothing away. He said it seemed to him like Mr Johnson had every right to do what he had done — the law was quite specific in cases such as this. Tough, yeah — his face was still blank as he shrugged

— but there it was.

Don Gabazo said: 'You should know, Marshal Kane, that in the West the strict letter of the law ees not always practical.'

'Cain't yuh get your water someplace else? From one o' your other neighbours?'

'I should have to cross Double W land to do that. I can't get past the wire. The stretch of land that Mr Johnson has had fenced off was the only place where I could get water without my steers wandering across a wide stretch of Double W land. Mr Johnson's late son left it unfenced for that reason.'

'Yeah, an' look what he got fer it.'

'I had nothing to do with the death of Colly Johnson,' said the old Mexican with dignity.

'Mebbe not. But you were all against him weren't you?'

'No one molested him.'

'The old man figures it wuz through you people — all of you — that his son died. I guess you cain't blame him f'r tryin' to get his own back — legally too.'

'The fact remains . . . '

Don Gabazo paused. His son, who up till then had been standing beside him in silent rage, had started forward.

A gun appeared in the hand of Flash Kragar. The two young men, the dark Mexican and the yellow-haired Texan, measured each other.

The latter said: 'It's mighty dangerous tuh move sudden like that, *hombre*.'

The young Mexican turned his hot dark eyes on the marshal.

'If you don't do something about this, *señor*,' he said, 'we will.' Then he turned to the old man at his side. 'Come, father, we will haggle no more.'

The old man saw the point of his son's new-found wisdom and turned away. No, it seemed useless to haggle further.

The marshal said: 'Oldtimer — I'd make sure that son o' yours don't do anythin' drastic that might start a heap o' trouble. I'll see Mr Johnson f'r yuh.'

Don Gabazo bowed. 'Thank you.'

'He won't do anything,' said Pedro when they got outside. 'He's Johnson's hired thug.'

'We will give them all a leetle more time,' said Don Gabazo. He was a disappointed old man. The much-vaunted US law had let him down.

'And then what?' said Pedro. 'You'd better hand things over to me, father.'

'What will happen then? Nothing by bloodshed.' The old man's voice was harsh. In his younger days, when his lovely wife was alive, he had fought Indians and bandits to carve himself his little empire on the banks of the Rio — and to gain peace. Goodwill with his neighbours had been sweet, he had grown old in the lap of contentment. He had bitterly resented the coming of Colly Johnson and the innovation of the Double W and its arrogant fences — Pedro had wanted to do something about that too — but Colly had not fenced off the creek. Nothing was changed really. The old man leaned back once more in his complacent twilight . . . Was all this to be split apart, shattered by a grief-crazed old Easterner?

'If nothing is done we will seek the law at San Antonio,' said Don Gabazo.

'The law!' spat Pedro. 'What can the law do? Of what use to us is this law? It can do nothing. This time, father, we will have to do it ourselves.'

The day was very hot and thirsty cattle milled and bawled on the range. Their eyes were beginning to bulge, their tongues to show a little. They lacerated their hides against the cruel barbs of the fence as they tried frenziedly to push through to the water they could see, and smell so maddeningly. But the fence had been built to withstand such an onslaught and merely sagged a little, sinking its cruel teeth into the flesh of the most persistent beasts until they lumbered away, bawling with pain and pestered by the particularly loathsome kind of fly that abounded in the heat and loved to sup their fresh blood.

Double W men, keeping a look-out by the creek, saw *vaqueros* in the distance but none of them came even within hailing distance. At the other side of the range a few cattle had bloated themselves out with the semi-poisonous salt-water of the Rio and were going mad, to the peril of their fellows. Several of them had to be shot.

Extracting a promise from his son that he would not do anything unfortunate while his father was away, Don Gabazo rode, with two men, to the Double W ranch house.

Emmanuel Johnson was 'indisposed' and could not see him. Lawyer Hiram Bloomfield saw the visitors. He spread his little plump hands apologetically. He could do nothing. As a lawyer he knew Mr Johnson was quite within his rights in fencing-off the water . . . Mr Johnson was a businessman. No, if Don Gabazo chose to put it that way, humanity did not enter into Mr

Johnson's calculations of this kind. Perhaps they would come to some arrangements later on.

'Meanwhile my poor cattle can die of thirst,' said the old Don. He rose, losing his temper. His two men moved alongside him.

Little Bloomfield started back in alarm. The bruiser Pilson took his place.

'Don't start any funny business,' he growled.

Behind him came Brad Ruston, the foreman, his arm in a sling, the other hand gripping a gun. Then Bronc Malone and two more Double W gunnies.

Don Gabazo bowed his shoulders. He turned to his men and motioned them away.

He turned suddenly at the door. 'The marshal said he would come and see you.'

'The marshal has not been here today,' said Pilson.

That night a Double W guard at the

creek fell backwards with a strangled cry as the flat report of a rifle-shot echoed over the mesa. His comrades elevated their guns, looking round. Another one turned to meet a slug squarely in his forehead. The man who could shoot in that muddy half-light must be a marksman par excellence. As one man, the rest of the guards threw themselves flat. The small bunch of steers that had been bawling outside the wire since sundown began to move slowly forward. Lying flat on the back of one of them, Pedro Gabazo, finest rifle-shot this side of the Rio, ejected another shell from his Lee-Enfield automatic and looked for another target. Behind the cover of the steers his men crept forward in crouching positions.

'That beef,' said one of the Double W men. 'It don't seem natural the way its moving. Let's drive 'em back.'

He fired a couple of shots at the advancing bunch, bringing one steer tumbling to the grass. Pedro who had

168

got a bead on the dark flat shadow from whence came flashes, squeezed trigger once more. The guard belched as if something had suddenly hit him in the guts, then he was terribly silent.

His companions shifted nervously. They had very little cover, nothing that a steel-jacketed rifle bullet could not plough through, and they could not see anything to shoot at except a few head of beef. There were nine men left now out of the dozen that had been posted there. Mr Johnson had insisted on a strong guard. A dozen had seemed mighty strong at the time — just for skulking behind barbed-wire in an area that afforded no cover for creeping marauders — but right now the luckless night-men wished there had been a hundred of them. Neither they nor the boss had contemplated a raid by a bunch of steers that seemed to throw lead from their very mouths — and with terribly deadly aim too, as was testified by the three silent figures which already lay there in the grass.

The guards strained their eyes and waited fearfully, each one of them scared to shoot and give his position away. The bunch of steers were almost on top of the wire now. Any of the shadows among them could be men. It was like fighting phantoms.

A couple of the guards lay silent in the bed of the creek. They were better hidden than their comrades but had not such a good view of what was going on outside the wire. However, as the cattle moved nearer, these two men got ideas and opened up.

'Rapid-fire!' screeched one of them who was, needless to say, an ex-soldier.

Heartened, the rest of them joined in. The front rank of steers received the full force of this barrage and they sagged on the wire. Then from in and around them, tongues of flame burst and withering lead sought out the men in the grass. Many of them were cut down without having a chance to fire again.

The wire fence twanged as it began

to part. The attacking *vaqueros* were getting to work on it with wire clippers. The cattle pushed and bawled, climbing over the carcases of those who had fallen before them. They were frantic now that the strange, painful thing that kept them from the precious water was gradually disappearing. The first bunch broke through.

The guards who still remained got up and ran for their horses, which were ground-hitched some distance away. They were picked off one by one with unhurried markmanship. Only four of them, one wounded in the hip, managed to get on their horses, and galloped madly away.

'We shan't catch them now,' said Pedro. 'Let them go.'

'They'll bring the whole bunch down on us,' said one man.

'That would have to happen sooner or later,' Pedro told him. 'It might as well be now. We want to keep them away from the hacienda . . . All of you volunteered for thees job without the knowledge of my father. Are you willing to go with me all the way?'

'We are, Pedro' . . . '*Sí* . . . *Sí*.' Even the grumbling one was game.

'We will get our horses first, then I will tell you my plan.'

When a strong force of Double W riders swept down to the creek, where a sizeable herd of thirsty steers milled now, they were met by a withering blast of fire from the rear of the herd. The exchanges were hot and furious as the Double W men began to encircle the herd.

The Mexican bunch was outnumbered and had to retreat, which was just how it had been planned by the astute Pedro. While the Double W men were extricating themselves from the mass of bawling cattle, the marauders got a good start. They were chased over the border via the Mal Rio Bridge and lost themselves in the hills which they knew so well.

It was morning when the weary hunters got back to home ground to be reviled by Emmanuel Johnson, who finally made himself ill with temper and weakly ordered the marshal to be sent to him.

When, later, Len Kane took a posse to the Gabazo hacienda, it was to find the old Don in a terrible state, worried over the sudden disappearance of his son and half of his men. Nothing could be done to him — even Kane had to admit that. He derived a little satisfaction out of making the old buzzard a damsight worse by telling him that the son and the missing men were wanted outlaws now with a noose awaiting them if they were caught.

Heavily-armed men rode the mesa and eyed the prowling lawmen with open hostility. A snooping deputy was discovered screaming, with the brand of a running-iron on his backside and no clue to the identity of the masked men who had treated him so.

The marshal knew the signs. He told Emmanuel Johnson that he had better drop his refencing schemes unless he wanted the whole territory on his neck. If that happened, Len Kane meant to pull from under pronto. He was hired to find Mert Scanlon — not handle a range war. Reluctantly, Johnson left the gap open and Don Gabazo's cattle continued to use the creek. But the crafty Eastern egotist had another ace up his sleeve. If the Mexican wanted rights to the water he must pay for them.

An agreement was duly drawn up and delivered by Hiram Bloomfield, accompanied by a sizeable bodyguard. Naturally, the old Don haggled but a broken man, now his son was lost to him, he soon gave in. Peace was all he wanted.

Jack Sharp was fit again, doing his work with the rest of the men, with only a plaster on his wounded side. But his looks were changed. A jagged white scar split the freckled mahogany of one side of his face, making the corner of one eye droop a little and giving his lips a sinister quirk. If he was homely before, now he looked a real hardcase.

Rumours reached his ears of how Bronc Malone was blowing around San Martini of nights, telling everybody how he made Jack Sharp, reputed to be real fast, back down. Of how Sharp was fit now but would not follow up his challenge and come out and fight. Why, the fellah hadn't been seen in town for weeks. He was skulking at the Horse V with his tail between his legs.

Pretty soon people began to believe all the loud-mouthed Double W top-hand told them. It was right, Jack Sharp hadn't been seen around much in town lately. It was said Malone had marked him for life, pistol-whipped him as if he were a cur. Any man who stood for that and did nothing about it was a yellow dog. Even some of Jack's own pardners began to look at him askance. But he went quietly on his inscrutable way. Arizona and Gyp, who were with him almost continually now, kept their own counsel too. They were somewhat puzzled at Jack's demeanour but they knew he was not yellow and they trusted him implicitly.

One cloudless morning the three of them were branding calves when Hank Bulger rode out to them.

The Old Man's face was unusually grave. He reined in his huge piebald directly in front of Jack.

'I've got some bad news for yuh.'

The scar-raced ranny looked up from his work.

'What's that boss?'

'Mert Scanlon's daid.'

Jack straightened up and braced his shoulders like a man who had just received a stinging blow across the eyes.

'How? Did they ketch him?'

The Old Man said: 'I've bin into town. The marshal told me. No, they didn't catch him. They found his body washed up on the shores of the Colorado. Seemed he musta fell into the river on the very stormy night we had awhile back. He wuz purty badly smashed up.'

'Air they sure it's him?'

'Yeh. His clothes, his build, altho' the face was badly battered. Everything else told 'em. They found his horse wandering loose too — further along the river.'

Jack shook his head slowly. 'So he didn't even have a chance to go out fightin'.'

'I'm sorry,' said the Old Man. 'But I guess maybe it wuz better that way. He ain't got any more blood on his hands . . . Jack — ef'n you'd like the rest of the day off — there's still some o' the boy's things back at the ranch. Ef'n . . . ' The hard-bitten old man paused in embarrassment.

'Thanks, boss,' said Jack. 'But I think I'll carry on right here.'

'Suit yourself, son.'

As the Old Man rode away, Jack turned slowly back to his work. For the rest of the day he was very silent.

He left the bunkhouse that night right after chow. Everybody left him alone. A man wanted to be just that way sometimes. They did not know that once outside he walked swiftly to the stables and saddled-up his horse.

Some time later a man slid up to Bronc Malone at the bar of the Golden Pesos Saloon and said: 'Jack Sharp's in town.'

'Pass the word tuh some o' the boys,' said the big tophand out of the corner of his mouth. 'Tell 'em tuh keep their eyes peeled.' And then — pretty well prepared for any eventuality — Malone turned, braced himself against the bar, and waited.

The word passed around and people began to move away from the centre of the floor. Some of them went outside and stood by the windows. It was too dark out on the street here to do any real shooting. Looked like it would have to be inside, beneath the garish lights of the Golden Pesos. Malone had certainly picked his position well. What a farce it would be if Jack Sharp passed right along. Malone would have to hunt the yellow dog.

Then the subject of all the speculation rode his horse down the main drag. He looked around him, saw the watching groups and noted the silence that greeted his arrival. In a shaft of light spearing from a window, his scar was like a white blaze on his face; the quirk of his lips made him look like he was enjoying a secret, sardonic joke.

He halted his horse outside the Golden Pesos and slid negligently from the saddle. He looped the reins over the hitchin'-rack and bowtied them . . .

'Evenin', folks,' he said to the silent group by the window.

'Evenin', Jack,' they said.

One said diffidently: 'Mighty sorry tuh hear about Mert, Jack.'

'Yeah, Mert had all the bad breaks,' said the scar-faced man.

He strode nonchalantly to the batwings and swung them apart. He went through them, then paused a little on the threshold of the Golden Pesos and looked about him. People began to fade just a little further away. Jack took a few more steps forward. His eyes, colder than usual, the one twisted queerly at the corner, seemed to be everywhere. Bronc Malone came away from the bar, his arms crooking. Jack's hands were by his sides, swinging a little as he walked. Everything was kind of slow and easy, but tension almost crackled in the air.

Then everything exploded at once.

Malone blurred into motion. Jack did not seem to pause in his stride but there was a little shuck as his irons cleared leather. Smoke wreathed his hips as the heavy Colts bucked and flamed. Malone's hands were glued to the butts of his weapons; they opened, spreading like claws, clutching at air. A terrible look of surprise contorted his broad face. It brought a glow to his eyes which just as swiftly faded, leaving them blank and sightless. His adam's apple jerked as he gulped twice.

Even as he was falling another man stepped out of the crowd. Haste proved his undoing for even as he fired the shot that plucked harmlessly at the shoulder of Jack's shirt, the scar-faced man was triggering again. The second man gave an awful cry, staggered forward, and collapsed on his face, almost on top of the spread-eagled form of Malone.

Jack Sharp's guns weaved, menacing the room as he backed away. He parted the batwings with a crash of his bootheels, spinning his body as he went through. As he reached the sidewalk a figure blurred in the road-way. Jack dropped on one knee, triggering once more. A slug took his hat off. The man in the roadway ran forward on his toes for a few steps then flopped down. He lay squirming feebly.

The watching people scattered for cover as two more guns opened up in the shadows opposite. Jack threw himself flat. A slug thunked into a porch-post. A horse on the hitching-line squealed in agony. Along in the shadows on the same side of the road as Jack, other guns opened up. It sounded like their owners were fanning the hammers. Over the road a man cried out in agony. Another man left the sidewalk and began to run. He paused in midstride as if he had suddenly remembered something, then he crumpled.

Two figures moved out of the shadows and joined Jack.

'Git up ol' timer,' said little Gyp. 'Yuh cain't lay down there all night.'

Jack rose. He looked surprised. 'Thanks, boys,' he said. All three of them made for their horses.

'The Ol' Man thought mebbe you'd ride,' said Arizona. 'We figured we'd come along with yuh.'

'All right,' said Jack. 'Let's git going.'

9

'Something To Remember Us By'

A few days later, three rannies walked through the gates of the Texas Ranger Post on the outskirts of San Antonio. One was small and kinda wizened, one lean and redheaded, the other sandy-haired and of medium build. A terrible scar on his face gave him a real mean look. This latter asked a lounger, with gun-slinger written all over him, where they had to go to enlist in this shebang.

The lounger jerked a thumb. 'Round the corner — Major's office,' he said laconically. But it was with speculative eyes that he watched the three men as they thanked him and walked on. Yessir, they looked real salty hellions. If they had a clean bill of health, the Major would be real glad to see 'm. Good rangers were mighty hard to find along the border nowadays. Gambling and panhandling paid more and was a damsight easier.

Fiery, emaciated Major Cliff Gaggo bawled 'Come in' to the knock at his door. His little sharp blue eyes, peering from his thin wrinkled face like currants from a rock-bun, keenly appraised the three men who entered.

They stated their business. He showed no emotion but began to bark questions in the voice, toned low a little now, that made raw recruits jump out of their skin. These were prospective recruits — but far from raw.

One of his main questions was shot at them with dramatic suddenness. Sometimes this surprise method brought forth the right answer.

'You on the run?'

'Nope,' said Jack. 'Not as we know of.'

'That's a recent scar. How did you get it?'

Jack told him the whole story — even the ending, of how he and his pards paid off the score — and double. Self-defence. And not a bit of doubt about it.

'Straight of you to tell me,' said the major with his first sign of affability.

'I'd guess you'd find out anyway,' said Jack.

'I would that.' The major paused. Then he said:

'Stay in town for a couple of days. I'll send for yuh if I want yuh. If you leave town, I'll know you've changed your minds. In the meantime, I'll be making enquiries.'

'All right.' This was all the change the three pardners got. But they judged it favourable: unless something happened to ball up the works.

It was in San Antonio that night that they first heard news of the mysterious bandit-gang that had suddenly descended on their old hunting-grounds, the San Martini territory, had run off with two hundred head of the Double W ranch's prize Herefords, killed two nightriders and almost started a prairie-fire. It was said that the leader of the band was a tall, dark man; a swashbuckler with a curly moustache and an imperial. He reminded garrulous oldtimers of Jack Gomez, the romantic scourge of the border of a decade ago.

The next day, sooner than they expected, Major Gaggo sent for the boys. A lean, taciturn, two-gun man accosted them in a honky-tonk and led them to the old soldier's office.

He was abrupt. 'You're in,' he said. 'You haven't changed your minds have yuh?'

They shook their heads. 'All right. We'll begin to teach you how we do things around here. You might be salty hellions in your neck of the woods but the ability to shoot fast and straight isn't the only thing a ranger needs. He needs to do a hell of a lot of straight thinking before he starts shooting. He must keep his temper — and all personal thoughts out of any of his dealings. When he makes a decision he's got to be right; his life and the life of others may depend on it . . . Right — I've finished preaching. You've got a lot to learn but I think you'll be all right. You'll disappoint me if you're not. Now get down to the chuckhouse and see Bill Rordan; he'll put you right.'

Bill Rordan proved to be a giant Irishman. He fixed them up with chow first of all — enough of it to choke a hippopotamus, and served up by a jasper who looked like one. A little later, after Bill had passed his makings round, he found them a badge apiece.

'Don't pin it where everybody can see it,' he said. 'Sometimes you might have to hide it in your boot or someplace.'

It seemed like the three men had everything else they needed.

But the badge alone did not make them rangers. 'It's what you've got in your noddle too,' said Bill with a sage wag of his bullet head. 'There ain't much discipline — 'cept what you make yourself. An' a good ranger learns how tuh discipline himself.' Then as if he thought he had said too much, and was in danger of an enthusiastic spiel, Bill shut up like a clam.

The three pardners soon got to know the boys of the post, although there was a shifting personnel: the Jim who occupied a bunk one evening was often superseded by a Tom on the next. The three recruits were answering questions all day long; cunning questions that tested their general knowledge, their tracker's and wood craft, their overall knowledge of the West and its varied peoples to the utmost. They had target practice too, both with rifle and pistol, and tests of skill and speed. At these latter they were as proficient as any man in the camp. In fact, it was said of Jack Sharp that he could beat the draw of anybody there.

The boys were taken out singly, by old rangers, on sorties into the surrounding Western terrain. Outwardly they were just friendly jog-trots, but they were also tests for the new recruits. Testing woodcraft, the quickness and clearness of their eyes, the handling of their horses over specially-picked obstacles; and other suitable and practical things. Gradually, but very surely, they made the grade.

News came to them from time to time about further depredations by the bandits in the San Martini territory. The Pinwheel ranch had had a barn burnt down, the Horse V lost a string of good horses, Don Gabazo lost a dozen head of steers and the rest were driven on to Double W land, through wire that had been churned down as if by an express train. Superstitious talk was still going on about the leader of the band being a reincarnation of the fabulous Gomez. More level-headed people scoffed at this idea: most probably the leader was not even the moustached and imperialled dandy he was supposed to be. Maybe that was just a tale, too — who had actually seen him anyway? Why, the skunks struck so swiftly and vanished again so miraculously to their hideout over the border that nobody had a chance to take a good look at them. The three ex-Horse V rannies had been of the opinion that the outlawed Pedro Gabazo and his men were responsible for the raids, being as the first one had concentrated solely on the Double W. But now they were dubious — surely Pedro would not raid the ranches of his own father and his friends . . .

Jack Sharp had been at the Ranger Post about ten days when he was taken out on his first assignment by a hardbitten oldster, a founder member of the bunch, named Cal Brackson. They were bound for the Brasos country, and as they rode, old Cal told his partner why.

'Did yuh ever know a *hombre* named Lemmy Buxton?'

'Yeah,' said Jack. 'Slightly. Met him in San Antonio a few times a while back. Ranger wasn't he?'

'Yeah,' said Cal. 'Wal, a few weeks ago he was sent along the Brasos after a killer named Joe Ems. He ain't bin heard of since. The major figures maybe Ems bushwhacked him. That's what we gotta find out. An' catch Joe Ems at the same time if he's still around. I'm kinda worried about Lemmy myself. He's a good ranger — ef'n he'd gotta keep chasing Ems he'd let us know some how.' Cal shook his greying head under its filthy Stetson. 'I'm afeard sump'n must've happened to him.'

The two rangers reached blustering Waco on the Brasos River. There, a surprise awaited them. Joe Ems, a well-known character here, had fallen off a cliff some weeks ago and broke his neck.

'Wal, that takes keer o' him,' said Cal, after ascertaining that it was, without a shadow of doubt, the wanted killer that was buried in the local Boot Hill. 'Now tuh find Lemmy. What in tarnation could've happened to him.'

The missing ranger was harder to trace. He evidently had not divulged his real identity to anyone in Waco. They could only call around giving descriptions of him — describing him as a friend of theirs they were on the lookout for. Finally they hit upon the boarding house where he had stayed for a couple of nights. The would-be coy, middle-aged landlady remembered him well. A tall, dark, handsome young man. He had left Waco above a fortnight ago and she hadn't seen him since. Other boarders corroborated that statement. Len Barker he had called himself.

The two rangers sought for further leads, but it was as if they had come plumb up against a brick wall. Lemmy Buxton — alias Len Barker — seemed to have vanished into thin air.

They travelled further: Fort Worth, Dallas, along the Trinity River. Then back again along the Brasos and so on, retracing their steps, taking in Austin. There they had hopes once more. A few people thought they had seen a young man answering to Lemmy's description, passing through a week or so ago. Yeah, yeah, like as if he was making for

San Antonio . . . But between Austin and San Antonio, Lemmy had disappeared as if the earth had opened up and swallowed him.

Reluctantly, the two rangers confessed themselves beaten and returned to the post. Maybe Lemmy would turn up — but they held no great hopes of that possibility.

'If he wuz daid, surely we'd know?' said Cal Brackson. 'Looks tuh me like he's quit the force altogether an' hightailed for a new line of country. The Major ain't gonna like that . . . ' The Major didn't.

Jack met up again with Arizona and Gyp, and they swapped yarns. Things hung fire for them at the post for the next couple of days, then the Major sent for all three of them.

As was his custom he got to the point right away.

'You boys came from the San Martini country didn't yuh?'

They affirmed they did.

'I guess you've heard o' this bunch o'

193

border-hellions who are terrorizing that region?'

They certainly had.

'I want you to go back there an' look things over. You know the country well — you're just the men for the job.'

'Marshal Kane ain't gonna like us goin' back, Major,' said Gyp. 'Particularly Jack here.'

'Marshal Kane can't do a thing,' said the old soldier harshly. He evidently had no great opinion of the notorious lawman. 'I'll give you a letter for him. See if you can get him to co-operate — don't get in his hair too much. It'd probably be best if you do not divulge the fact of your new status to anybody else but the law. Start back at your old jobs if you like — if you can trust your old boss, tell him the truth in confidence — but don't forget you're working for Uncle Sam now . . . I'll rely on you to keep in touch with me. Collect everything you want and get going right away.

'And good luck to you,' the old

194

soldier called as they left his office.

'He's a real decent ol' galoot 'spite of his bark,' was little Gyp's verdict.

★　★　★

The Double W ranch-buildings were shrouded in darkness. Out front, stragglers from the nearest herd of beef boomed their melancholia. A night-rider whistled to his pard and, far out in the hills, a coyote yelped shrilly.

Across the mesa, approaching the back of the ranch house at a steady trot, came a bunch of horsemen. Their horses' hoofs looked enormous, freak-ish; they were padded with strips of cloth to deaden sound. All the men wore bandannas around the lower halves of their faces.

They halted a few hundred yards behind the ranch-buildings. The two foremost masked men, one of whom appeared to be the leader, were lean, upright in the saddle. They split away from the main group and made for the ranch house proper. The others, a sizeable bunch of them, began to surround the bunkhouse. They moved silently like phantoms in the dark night. Some of them slid from their horses, others remained mounted.

Three of them, after seeing a beckoning arm from one of the two men on foot by the back porch of the ranch house, joined them there. They spread out and stayed outside while the two men plunged into the shadows of the porch.

The slighter of the two got to work on a window with a thin-bladed knife. The bigger man followed. They stopped dead, getting their eyes accustomed to the darkness, and listening.

Then the first one opened a door and advanced purposefully down a passage. He seemed to know his way around the place. A gun glinted in each man's hand now. They turned a corner and began to ascend the stairs. The carpet, reaching up on to the wide landing, was soft and thick beneath their feet. This was the most palatial ranch house either of them had ever been in.

The first man tried the second door on the landing. He opened it and slid through.

Emmanuel Johnson had not slept well at all since coming West. The quietness of the open spaces, after the roar around his apartment in Chicago, got on his nerves. He dozed fitfully, his thin body hardly outlined beneath the sheets, his sharp-nosed visage upturned. His senses were not as acute as of yore. By the time he realized that someone else was in the room beside himself, the lean figure was beside his bed. There was another bigger figure nearer too.

Emmanuel opened his mouth to scream. A hand bearing a chloroformed pad pressed down over his mouth and nose. He spluttered and struggled a little, then went limp. The bigger man lifted him as if he had been a child. The other catfooted to the door, opened it and slid out.

A giant figure loomed up in the passage. 'Hey?' said Bruiser Pilson.

'Freeze,' said the shadowy gunman. 'Another sound and you die. Put up your hands.'

Pilson backed against the passage wall. Guns always scared him. He raised his hands. The other marauder came out of the room with his burden.

'We cain't leave him here,' he said, with a jerk of his head at Pilson.

Before the giant could duck or utter a sound the gunman stepped forward. The blue-steel of his gun flashed in the darkness. There was a dull crump. Pilson buckled at the knees. The gunman caught him and eased him to the floor. Even so he caused quite a bump.

The gunman followed his colleague down the passage. A door opened beside him and a little figure in a voluminous night-shirt came out.

'Help!' he screeched.

The gunman snarled and hissed something in Spanish. The muzzle of the gun was almost touching the folds of the white nightgown as the man squeezed the trigger. The report split the night apart like a cannon-shot. The echoes rumbled along the passage and rang down the stairs where the other man, with his burden, was turning to curse.

Hiram Bloomfield moaned slightly and crumpled up. The gunman left him — like a small bundle of washing on the landing. More doors were being flung open as the two men ran down the stairs. The one behind turned and, fanning the hammer of his gun, sent a stream of hot lead screaming behind him. Up there in the darkness a man yelped in agony.

By the time the pursuers retaliated the two murderers with their burden, were around the corner and running along the downstairs passage to the back-place.

Somebody hissed: 'Boss.' One of the men from outside was coming to meet them.

'Take this carrion,' said the tall man. 'An' get going.' He handed over the limp form of the old millionaire.

The man slung the featherweight burden across his shoulders as if it were a sack of meal and retraced his steps.

The two men followed him into the kitchen and then stopped. 'We'll give these bastards sump'n tuh remember us by,' said the bigger one, and shucked his two guns from their holsters.

The first pair of luckless waddies came around the corner from the stairs. At the kitchen door the big man dropped on one knee and thumbed the hammers methodically. The two men were cut down like ripe corn, one of them screaming horribly. There was quiet then, except for the faint slide of feet on the stairs.

The big man watched the faint upright line that was the corner of the stairs. His features, etched in the half-light were well-formed, aquiline. A jutting goatee beard pushed out the fringe of the bandanna around the lower half of his face. He thought he saw a movement and fired again. Then he turned away, slamming the kitchen door. The other man was at the window. He beckoned and the big man followed him through.

Up at the bunkhouse, voices were shouting. They ran towards them. Before they reached the place, gunfire began to crackle. A man ran out of a dark gap. Hoofs thundered behind him and a Colt boomed in the enclosed space. The man turned an almost complete somersault, twitched for a moment like a misshapen wounded bird, then lay still.

The horseman reined in before the two men. 'The punchers've come alive an' started cuttin' up rough,' he said.

'We gotta get goin',' said the big man. 'Round up the boys! Set fire tuh the place if you've got the chance, but don't take any risks. We don't want anybody tuh get caught.'

'Yeah, boss,' said the man. He turned

his horse and galloped back the way he had come.

Many of the luckless Double W men, still in various states of undress and alarm, were penned-up in the bunk-house under withering fire from the attackers. The most fortunate ones were those who had been awakened by the first shot at the ranch house and had run out to investigate. They had been cut down like so many clay pigeons: they sprawled in grotesque attitudes on the hard baked soil before the bunk-house. The attackers were utterly ruthless.

They were fanning out each side, working their way round to join their leaders who, now the main purpose of the raid had been accomplished, wanted to get started. They didn't want to risk leaving any wounded men, who could talk, behind them. Up till now the attackers had had only a couple of men wounded, and those pretty slightly: they had been tied to their horses and sent round the back.

From each corner, as they worked their way round, the raiders kept up a withering cross fire. Torches flared, describing fiery arcs in the air. One landed on the bunkhouse roof, rolled, and spluttered harmlessly to the ground in a shower of sparks. Another fell into the dried grass that clustered around the back, at the base of the building. It caught and travelled, a miniature edge of flame that gradually grew as it licked its way up the log walls.

Evidently the raiders had come prepared for an all-out sweep. Another flaming torch thudded on the back porch of the verandah, while a hail of lead kept at bay the few house-lackeys who were sniping, with little result, from there. Yet another torch crashed through a kitchen window. Smoke bellowed from the place as men frenziedly dashed water on the small conflagration. Another torch crashed on to the roof, rolled to the eaves and there stuck, tongues of flame darting from it, licking voraciously at tinder-dry timber.

'Come on,' bawled the leader of the bandits. 'Git goin.'

His men joined him. A last spatter of shots came from the burning building where men screamed and beat at the flames that threatened to consume them. This last tired gesture of defiance on the part of the surprised and panicked ranchmen surprisingly bore fruit: a rider in a very wide-brimmed sombrero toppled from his horse.

'Juan,' said another man and jumping from his horse fell on his knees beside the fallen man.

He looked up. 'He's dead, boss.'

'All right,' said the big man. 'Lash him to his horse. Hurry!'

The *vaquero* unhooked his riata and tied his dead comrade to his own saddle.

'Get moving,' said the big man. He swept his arm forward.

They galloped away. In the middle of them, tied face-downwards on a horse, Emmanuel Johnson began to moan feebly. Behind them the night sky was lit by a blazing inferno, tinting the clouds blood-red, proclaiming the tragedy of the Double W to everyone for miles around.

10

'Tomorrow and Forever'

Spears of morning sunlight made the dust-particles shimmer in Marshal Kane's improvized office in San Martini. The marshal, his eyes red-rimmed from lack of sleep, his hatchet-face drawn and grey, was sitting in a chair before the table. On the table was a small sheet of paper, a cup half-full of muddy coffee, and a pewter ashtray, over-flowing with cigarette stubs. On two chairs facing the marshal sat Flash Kragar and Sheriff Ep Blackson. They both looked like they had been doing a hell of a lot of rough riding for two or three nights in succession. They both dragged nervously at cigarettes.

Kane bent over a small sheet of grubby white paper on his table. He read out the capitals pencilled thereon:

WE HAVE EMMANUEL JOHNSON
SAFE WHERE NOBODY CAN FIND
HIM. DO NOT DO ANYTHING RASH.
WE WILL GET IN TOUCH WITH
YOU AGAIN IN THREE DAYS TIME.
THE GOMEZ BOYS.

'Jack Gomez!' burst out Sheriff
Blackson.

'Jack Gomez, hell!' snarled the
marshal. 'Jack Gomez has been daid f'r
years now. D'yuh think this is his ghost
or sump'n, like some o' these crack-
brained ol'timers?'

'No, of course not,' said the sheriff
licking his lips. 'Tho' the man who
leads them looks like Jack Gomez by all
accounts. Big dandy — moustache and
imperial and everthin' . . . '

'Did yuh ever see Jack Gomez?'

'N-no-o.'

'Wal, I did. He wuz like that all right.
Everybody knows what he wuz like.
Any sizeable younker could dress up to
look like him. Like I've said before
— this gink who leads the so-called

Gomez boys is none other than Pedro Gabazo . . . '

'But they raided Gabazo's rancho.'

'Jest a blind!' said Kane. 'They didn't do much harm did they? Jest run off a few head of cattle. I'll wager them cattle are back in their home pastures right now . . . Don't these people seem to have it in for the Double W more than any other place? Why — right now there jest ain't no Double W — due tuh them.'

'Pedro Gabazo ain't a big man,' said the sheriff.

'Oh, f'r Chris'sake!' said the marshal. 'He's lean ain't he? I guess he'd look tall on a hoss. Anyway, folks around here are so damn scared of this so-called ghost of Jack Gomez that if they did see him they'd probably think he wuz a dozen foot wide and sported a pair of wings.'

Flash Kragar, who up till now had listened silently to the conversation with a sardonic half-smile on his thin lips, suddenly sniggered. The marshal had not meant to be funny. He glared at his aide-de-camp. Flash rose and with a cigarette dangling from his lips crossed to the window and looked out . . .

Kane looked at the sheriff again. 'Why,' he said. 'That young Mexican skunk has been brought up along these border hell-spots. He wuz reared on legends such as the Gomez one. It's him all right. Who else could it be? He wuz chased over the border wasn't he? He had a grudge against Johnson and the Double W didn't he?'

The sheriff nodded his head jerkily each time a point was thrust home at him. His long face looked sourer than ever, his red eyelids drooped.

Suddenly, Flash Kragar said: 'Hey, Len!' in a startled high-pitched voice as if something had suddenly bitten him.

'Now what's the matter?'

Kragar was gawping out of the window as if he could see a parade of purple elephants coming down the street.

'Come here! Look who's here.'

Both the sheriff and the marshal joined him at the window.

'I didn't think they'd have the nerve,' said the marshal softly.

'Looks like they're comin' here too,' said the sheriff, mystified.

'All right,' snapped Kane. 'Away from the window. Back to your seats. Push your chair further back, Flash. If they do come in here an' start somethin', you know what to do.'

'Sure,' said Flash. Again he smiled his thin-lipped half-smile. A yellow-haired rattlesnake.

The clattering of hoofs stopped right outside. Boot-heels thudded on the porch. The door banged. The three waiting men heard the querulous voices of the landlady.

Then a man's voice said: 'Marshal Kane here?'

The landlady said something else. Boot-heels thudded nearer. Then somebody hammered the door.

'Come in,' called the marshal.

The door opened. Jack Sharp

entered, behind him his two pards, Arizona and Gyp.

'Wa-al — the prodigals return,' said Marshal Kane. There was no humour in his voice.

'Howdy, folks,' said Jack, coolly. 'Nice seein' yuh again.'

'Yeah, jest like ol' times,' grinned little Gyp.

The red-headed Arizona, who couldn't see any sense in this byplay, merely grunted.

'Sit down, boys,' said the marshal. 'What can I do f'r yuh — 'sides lockin' yuh up, I mean?'

Maybe he meant to be funny that time. Maybe he didn't. Nobody laughed anyway.

He indicated the long horsehair sofa that almost bisected the room. The three men sat down, their backs to Flash Kragar now.

Jack turned his head. 'Pull your chair forward, Flash,' he said. 'Join the pow-wow.'

The yellow-haired gunny hesitated

for a moment. The scarred face of the other man leered at him. Finally he drew up his chair. Sheriff Ep Blackson's sour visage smiled a little.

'How've yuh bin, boys?' he said.

'Oh, so-so.' Jack turned again to Kane. 'I've got a letter f'r you, marshal.'

Kane looked as surprised as his hawk-like face would allow.

'A letter? F'r me?'

Jack took it from his vest-pocket and tossed it on the table. Kane took it, slit the envelope with his thumb and extracted the small sheet of notepaper. He opened it, his eyebrows raising a little as he saw the official stamp at the top. The look of surprise grew as he read the missive.

Then he said: 'By all thet's holy — rangers!'

'Whassat?' said the sheriff.

'These three jaspers — they're Texas Rangers.'

'These three?' said the sheriff, mouth agape.

'Yeah, these three. This is a letter

from Major Gaggo at San Antonio, asking us to co-operate with them in endeavouring to catch the San Martini bandits.' The marshal's face suddenly split in a grin — a far from engaging one that made no difference to his cold eyes. 'So you've come tuh lay the ghost f'r us have you . . . ? Wal, he's all yours — here's the latest example of his hauntin'.' He tossed the other slip of paper across the table.

Jack took it and read it. Without comment, he passed it on to his pards. They read it and chucked it back on to the table. Then Jack said:

'When did this happen?'

'Last night. They took the ol' man out o' the ranch house — right from under the noses of his men, an' then tuh finish the job off they set the place on fire. Right now the Double W is purty near razed tuh the ground. Nine men daid.'

Even the hardbitten faces of the rangers revealed their shock at this news.

'Any leads a'tall?' said Jack. 'Any clues — any wounded or daid bandits?'

'Nothin',' said Kane. 'If they had any dead men they must've taken 'em with 'em.' He rose abruptly, his hawk-face blank. 'The sheriff'll tell yuh the rest. I gotta go upstairs.' He made for the door.

Without a word Flash Kragar followed him. Jack scowled, making his scarred face look ferocious. 'Marshal. We wouldn't like anybody else tuh know the real reason for our return here — an' that we're rangers. The major wouldn't like it.'

'No, I guess he wouldn't,' said Kane. Kragar closed the door behind them. The three men heard them clattering up the stairs.

Jack turned to the sheriff. 'Wal, Ep,' he said.

The lawman's face lightened a little. He had gotten used to playing second fiddle now, but he evidently preferred the company of the three rangers to that of the marshal and his side-kick.

He told them all he knew and of the marshal's theory that Pedro Gabazo was the pseudo Gomez.

'Seems likely,' said Arizona.

'I admit that,' said the sheriff — although while back he had, perversely tried to talk the marshal out of it. 'An' last night's little jamboree does kinda smack of greaser savagery.'

'You've seen old Don I reckon?'

'Yeah — cain't get nothin' out of him. The ol' buzzard's goin' tuh pieces. I guess he thinks his son's behind it all too.'

'But the ol' man's got nothin' tuh do with it himself.'

'If he has, he's a mighty fine actor.'

'Wal,' said Jack. 'I guess we'll ride an' get our ol' jobs back.'

'Yeah, ain't that the best way? Nobody's gonna be suspicious. We kin work under cover, that is if somebody don't give the show away.'

'You can count on me, boys,' said the sheriff soberly.

Old Hank Bulger was as surprised as anybody to see his three trouble-shooters back in the territory — and all in one piece too. Knowing that he was as true as steel, as well as being a naturally close-mouthed old skunk, the boys took him into their confidence.

He was highly delighted. 'Ef I can be of any material help a'tall, boys,' he said. 'You know you kin count on me. I'll admit that when them pesky bandits fust started their high jinks and the Double W got the worst of it, I wuz inclined to crow. But last night's caboodle was no joke — it was cold-blooded slaughter. An' whoever was responsible for it — whether it be Pedro Gabazo or Jack Gomez's ghost — oughta be burnt alive. The whole stinkin' bunch of 'em want exterminatin' . . . And,' he concluded, 'I'm tellin' yuh right now, boys — if you can get a lead on these people an' nose 'em out, I guess I can guarantee a sizeable bunch of fightin' men from here an' the Pinwheel, ef not the Gabazo spread, who'll be raring to ride with yuh tuh smoke 'em tuh Kingdom Come.'

'Well spoken, ol' timer,' said little Gyp as the indignant rancher stopped for breath.

'An' worth rememberin',' said Jack.

'I can even feel kinda sorry for that ol' buzzard the bunch've kidnapped,' said the Old Man.

'They probably mean to hold him to ransom,' said Jack. 'He'll pay it — with all his millions, a few odd hundred thousand'll be a mere drop in the ocean.'

'Wal, I hope they mean tuh let him go eventually,' said Hank, darkly. 'But I'm a-figuring they're more likely to do away with him so's he won't talk — whether they get their money or not. They're mighty keerful nobody don't recognize 'em — even in the dark — with their masks an' all.'

The boys learned from him that sightseers had been travelling down to the ruins of the Double W ranch all day, so a visit from them would not cause speculation. People who wondered about the return of the three waddies who had shot up Bronc Malone and his cronies that rip-snorting night in San Martini, could be told that the boys — who weren't no damn murderers anyway — had come back to work for their ol' boss. An' he was mightily glad to have them back. That was simple enough.

'Thank you, boss,' carolled the boys as they galloped away.

They breasted a rise and gazed across the mesa towards where the palatial Double W ranch-buildings used to stand. They were shocked at the blackened smear that spread across the landscape in that old spot. They trotted their horses down the slope towards it. A few work-shy waddies were lounging around, smoking and speculating. They greeted the new arrivals guardedly, little wrinkles of anxiety on their faces, but intimidated by the grim looks of these three, now notorious, trouble-busters, they asked no questions.

The three men skirted the ruins: the brick-foundations of the long bunk-house, the blackened patches that were the only signs left of the cookhouse, the stables and other outhouses and barns. The only edifice left standing was an old feed-barn by the corral and even that, like the corral-fence, was scorched and blackened. A pitiful framework remained of the big, once magnificent, two-storeyed ranch house. The rangers learned that three men had perished in there: the bruiser, Pilson, the little lawyer — who had been shot before-hand, the slug was found among his charred bones — and one house-lackey. The Johnsons' Western empire was no more.

'This'll tell us nothin',' said Jack.

'The sheriff said he'd gone all over it,' said Arizona.

'I wasn't no lover of the Johnsons an' their hangers-on,' said Gyp, softly. 'But some of the Double W boys wuz jest waddies. I'd like to get my hands on the skunks that did this.'

'I guess we're all hoping to,' said Jack. He turned his horse abruptly. 'Come on.'

'Wait a minute,' said the sharp-eyed Arizona. 'What's thet skulking jasper got. He's bin rooting among the ashes on the edge o' the ranch house thar — he's picked something up.'

He indicated a furtive-looking gent who was tucking something into the pocket of his filthy jeans.

As the three men approached the man, whom they recognized as one of San Martini's worst scroungers, he looked up at them and smiled weakly.

'Howdy, boys.'

'What've yuh got there, Breezy?' said Jack.

'Why — nuthin', Jack.'

'Hand it over.'

' 'Tain't nuthin', Jack.' Breezy tried to look innocent.

'Give it to me,' snarled the ranger. When he scowled, his scarred face was enough to intimidate anybody — and Breezy was very poor stuff.

'It's jest a little trinket, Jack,' he bleated.

He brought his hand out of his jeans-pocket and held it out, palm upwards. On the grimy surface, glittering as the sun tantalized it, was a gold medallion.

Jack took it and scrutinized it. One side of it was blank. The other had an inscription. Jack read it out: a Spanish phrase meaning: 'Tomorrow and Forever.' Beneath was a name, Delores Montez, and a date.

'It's a mighty old piece ain't it,' said little Gyp.

'It is,' said Jack. 'An' one o' the finest lumps of pure yeller metal I've ever handled.'

He slipped it into his vest-pocket. 'Thanks, Breezy,' he said, sardonically.

'Don't mention it, Jack,' said the scrounger and shuffled off.

'Ef one of our bandit friends dropped this, it's suttinly a clue,' said Jack. 'The on'y one we've got so far.'

Just how valuable a clue it was to prove, they were pretty soon to discover.

As they moved away from the ruins a bunch of men approached with a prisoner in their midst.

It was Pedro Gabazo.

The three rangers rode up. 'We found him skulkin' around,' said one of the men.

Jack had a sudden hunch. 'It must've bin something mighty important to make you risk your neck coming down here alone,' he said. 'Wuz you lookin' fer sump'n? Sump'n that might give you away? Were you lookin' fer this, Pedro?'

He whipped the medallion from his pocket and stuck it under the Mexican's nose, but Pedro was not to be caught off his guard that easily. He remained mute and sullen.

Jack turned to his pards. 'Better take him into town, boys; I've got a hunch. I'm gonna ride to the Gabazo hacienda.'

Half-an-hour's hard riding got him there. He was ushered immediately into the presence of the old Don. He tried shock tactics again. He whipped the gold medallion from his pocket once more. 'This is yours isn't it, Don George?' he said.

The old man's face went white with emotion. He blurted out: 'It was my wife's. I gave it to her on our wedding eve. My son wore it around his neck . . . ' He drew in his breath with a gasp.

'Pedro! What has happened to him?'

'Nothing yet,' said Jack grimly. Then his voice softened a little. Maybe it would be better for the old man if the boy was already dead. 'I'm afraid I've got some bad news f'r you, Don George,' he said.

Jack Sharp rode from the Gabazo hacienda with bitter gall in his heart, leaving behind him a broken old man. The sandy-haired, scarfaced trouble-shooter made a solemn vow: it was his duty as a man, as well as a ranger, to wipe out that loathsome nest of border hellions. He thought again of the broken wreck behind him who had once been a proud Don. The old man who had once had a son. Jack Sharp vowed that that dirty son would talk turkey if he had to tear his heart out to make him.

So deep was he in his savage thoughts that he did not at first see the other rider who was cutting diagonally across the mesa to meet. The rider was almost on top of him before he became aware of it. He looked up, his hand instinctively dropping to his hip. Then he relaxed. It was Judy Hodgeson.

'Hallo, Jack,' she said, boyishly. 'Glad to see you back.'

Her blue eyes were warm, her face flushed by her ride. Jack had a queer constricted feeling in his throat as he looked at her.

His articulation seemed almost painful to him as he said: 'Hallo, Judy. How are you?'

'Fine thanks. And you?'

'Cain't grumble.'

'Mind if I ride along with you?'

'Good gosh no.' Then as if startled by his own vehemence, Jack shut his mouth like a trap.

Judy swung her horse alongside him. The usual commonplace greetings were over now. She was silent too, but, in the manner of women, she could not keep silent for very long. She said:

'Mr Bulger rode over to our place and told us you were back.'

'Did he tell you why we were back?' Jack's tone was unwontedly brusque.

The girl looked puzzled. 'What do you mean? Only that you and Arizona and Gyp had come back to work for him. I — I can't understand why you left.'

'You thought I ran out.'

'N-No, Jack. If you'd done that, you'd've never come back, but you could have stayed.' Her voice was suddenly metallic. 'I'm not a child, Jack. I know that what happened in San Martini that night — it just had to happen. You fought fairly — you, and Arizona and Gyp, and you had the whole territory with you. Nobody could've done anything I mean — that terrible marshal or his partner — or anybody.'

'I kinda figured that,' said Jack. 'No, that ain't the only reason I went. I — I had sort of made up my mind beforehand.' The girl looked up into the scarred face with the lips now tightly closed. Jack did not look at her. He looked straight ahead.

The girl said: 'It isn't something you don't want to tell me is it?' Then more softly. 'You know — you can tell me anything.'

'Wa-al.'

'All right,' she said. 'Keep your beastly secret.'

He looked at her, startled. There was a little twinkle in her blue eyes.

Their horses were flank to flank. He reached out a hand and awkwardly grasped the pommel of her saddle.

'Judy. I . . . Oh, hell!'

'Yes?' she said.

'Excuse my language.'

'Never mind your language,' she shot at him. 'Cuss as much as you like, but tell me what you've got to tell me.'

He took his hand from the saddle and sat up straight.

He said: 'Mebbe first of all I'd better tell you the real reason for me an' Arizona and Gyp coming back tuh this territory.'

'All right, I'm listening.'

So he told her all of it. When he finished, she said: 'So you left San Martini to join the Texas Rangers?'

'Wa-al. Partly.'

'Jack Sharp,' she said. 'Look at me. Come on, look at me — I don't mind your battle scars.'

He turned to face her. Her blue eyes were very warm and soft. She said: 'Did you leave San Martini because of me?'

'Gosh,' he burst out involuntarily. 'How did you know?'

'You poor manly fool,' she said with a little crooked smile. 'Don't you know women can sense those things . . . But why, Jack — why did you leave? Why didn't you speak?'

He looked at her in amazement. His answer was broken. 'You loved Mert Scanlon. He wuz my best friend, even tho' he had gone . . . Don't yuh see? I couldn't! Anyway I thought it wuz hopeless . . . Judy — You don't mean . . . ?'

'You fool,' she said and she sounded almost angry. 'I never loved Mert Scanlon. I was fond of him — yes. He was an amusing companion. But — Oh, Jack . . . ' Tears glinted on her lashes. 'Didn't you know? Couldn't you see? It's always been you . . . my old pard — ever since I was a girl in pigtails. I've always loved you — you strong, silent, adorable fool. Oh, Jack . . . ' Next moment she was crying on his shoulder.

He had never seen her cry before. Even as he stroked her soft blonde hair and made little incoherent murmurs of happiness, he paused to think on what queer critturs women were.

11

'Bad Hombre!'

Jack's ruthlessness had left him. He was in a dazed frame of mind when he entered San Martini and in no shape to put a prisoner through a merciless question routine. Consequently, it was perhaps all for the best that he found a message from Major Gaggo delivered by express, asking him — and only him — to return to San Antonio *pronto*!

Considering he had only recently arrived at San Martini, he was rather mystified by the Major's command — for such it was. However, he bade a surprisingly fond *adios* to Arizona and Gyp — they thought he'd got too much firewater from someplace — and, after filling his water canteen and shoving a package of sandwiches in his saddle-bag set out.

It was pretty late when he reached San Antonio. However, there was still a light in the major's office. The old soldier was waiting for him.

'What's the matter,' he snapped. 'Your horse break a leg?'

'I got here as quick as I could, Major.'

'All right — all right.' The peppery old soldier waved an impatient hand. Then said abruptly: 'You knew Mert Scanlon didn't you?'

'He wuz my best friend.'

'You're the man I want then.'

Still mystified, Jack wondered if the old goat had been sure of that before he sent for him all the way from San Martini.

The Major said: 'D'you know Panhandle Jones's livery-stable just off Main Street.'

'Yes, suh.'

'Well, I want you to go down there. He's got plenty to tell you. When he's finished, I want you to act on it. Or at least act on it first thing tomorrow morning ... I ought to lock the old skunk in jail — but I guess that wouldn't do any good ... All right — don't stand there! Get and see Jones.'

As he left the office, Jack was rather peeved, as well as mystified. Why had the major asked him about Mert Scanlon? He remembered suddenly that Panhandle had known Mert pretty well, too. He hurried down the main drag to his destination.

When he entered the stable, old Panhandle came out of the shadows.

'Major Gaggo sent me,' said Jack.

'All right, son,' said the old man. 'C'mon in the kitchen an' set down.' He led the way.

When Jack left the stables almost an hour later, he was a sadder and wiser man. He knew a lot of things that he had not known before. Perhaps the most startling fact of all was the truth about the identity of the son of the fabulous Jack Gomez. He realized now that although he had been Mert

Scanlon's best friend, he had never really known him. Nobody had ever really known Mert — not even that old-timer back there who had been his father's comrade. Jack figured he maybe knew now what had happened to Ranger Lemmy Buxton, but he found it hard to face the full realization, and his mind kept evading the issue. He spent a very troubled night, tossing in his bunk at the Ranger Post.

Next morning, just after dawn, after a scrappy breakfast which tasted like sawdust on his tongue, he set out once more for San Martini. Something told him all his problems would be solved for him ere long. He could not turn back. He was not sure he wanted to. Something inside him pushed him on, and he realized it would keep pushing him until he knew all the answers.

He rode hard, and was streaming with sweat and his horse was lathered when they reached San Martini.

He found Arizona and Gyp with the sheriff in his office. He learnt that nothing more had occurred in his absence. The sullen prisoner at the back still refused to open his trap, despite the pretty rough handling the marshal and his side-kick had given him.

'That yaller-haired younker Flash an' young Pedro really oughta get together,' said Gyp. 'They're so much alike.'

'Yeah, that Flash's a cruel bastard,' said Arizona. 'He wanted tuh burn the greaser's eyes out.'

'Mebbe you can make him talk, Jack,' said Sheriff Blackson. The scarfaced ranger figured that right now maybe he was in a position to tell Pedro a few things he did not know, but the young Mexican held the most important secret: the position of the Gomez Boys' hideout and where they were keeping Emmanuel Johnson.

He went into the cell-block and down the passage to the cell that held Pedro. The young Mex was sitting on his bunk staring moodily at the floor. His face was hardly recognizable, so puffed and battered was it. The marshal and his boy certainly played rough.

Pedro's plum-coloured check shirt was torn in a dozen places. Even one of his trouser legs was torn. The breast of his shirt was wide-open and, as he looked up, a livid bruise showed at the base of his neck. His thin lips, puffed a little at one corner, were clamped tight. His eyes glared at Jack. One of them was thinner than the other, a jagged line of dried blood ran from the corner of it.

'You gonna tell us what we want to know, Pedro?' said Jack.

The young Mexican did not answer. He dropped his head and began to look at the floor again.

Jack tried cajoling, then feeling as low as a snake's belly, he tried to play on the man's emotions by mentioning his old father, but he needn't have felt any shame. Jack smiled sardonically: Pedro didn't give a damn for his father. The ranger went on to threats — he almost dangled the noose in front of the prisoner's eyes.

But Pedro would not say a word, and

towards the end, Jack found himself half-admiring the fellow's guts.

He went back into the office.

Some time later, Kane and his side-kick entered. Both men's faces looked wolfish, their eyes cold. They greeted Jack surlily.

'Has that greaser talked?' said the marshal.

'Nope.'

'Give me the keys, sheriff.'

Silently, Blackson handed them over. 'Come on, Flash,' said the marshal, and they passed into the cell-block.

A few seconds later the folks in the office heard the cell-door clang shut. Then the growling voices of the lawmen began to sound, rising and falling, but indistinct through the closed door.

A little later there were dull thuds and smacks. The sound of blows — terrific blows — for the sound of them to travel like they did.

Then, suddenly, there was complete silence.

'What the hell air they up to now?'

said Sheriff Blackson, licking dry lips.

The silence dragged leadenly like the longest day. The men in the office were tense. Then, cutting the atmosphere as if it were a physical thing, came a half-stifled cry of pure agony: the first sound that Pedro Gabazo had uttered since his capture.

Sheriff Blackson went white. Then he crossed the room, opened the door of the cell-block and went through. A few moments later he returned. Kane and Kragar were with him. Behind them there was silence. There had been silence since that terrible cry.

Jack Sharp said: 'Yuh haven't killed him have yuh?'

'It might be better for him if we had,' said the marshal. 'People in the town are bi'ling-up f'r a lynching jamboree.'

'Mebbe we'd better get prepared for it then,' said Jack.

'Did the boy talk?' said little Gyp softly.

'No — not a thing.'

The sheriff went out by the side-door. He returned with a pitcher of water and passed into the cell-block once more.

★　★　★

At twilight there was a brooding stillness over San Martini. Little knots of men gathered in the single, cart-rutted main street and talked and smoked. Their voices were rumbling undertones in the hot stillness — now and then one would rise shrilly in a curse or denunciation, then stop short suddenly as if its owner was ashamed of himself. But as the night got darker and lights began to appear in the windows of the nightspots, the rumbling under-tone got steadily louder. The men began to file into the biggest saloon: Tubby La Rue's Golden Pesos.

Tubby, behind his bar, with another bartender beside him watched them with his little sleepy eyes. The orders came fast: some of the men tipped the liquor back as if it were spring-water.

Tubby turned his head and spoke softly to the bartender at his side. The man slid away through the door behind the bar with a message for the law. The lynch-talk was getting wilder. Pretty soon it would boil-up into action. The law listened and acted accordingly.

After heated arguments and one fight in the saloon, the mob, vociferating loudly now, began to spill out into the street. All they needed was a leader, someone to spur them on. Once they got moving, the man, whoever he was, could take a back-seat. Once they started, nobody would be able to stop them. All they needed was that one spark to start the conflagration.

It came from a drunken gambler known as Frisco Phil.

He was an experienced con-man who had harangued bigger crowds than this back at the Golden Gates. A bellyful of liquor made him as big as a horse and he was game for anything.

'Torches!' he yelled. 'That's what we

want — torches!'

Others took up the cry. 'Torches! Make a pageant of it.' Flaming brands of torn firewood and tarred rope were soon being waved frenziedly above the heads of the mob.

Frisco Phil, a torch in his own hand, mounted a wagon and held up a long arm for silence. His lean, pale face was not unhandsome; the flickering light lent it an almost noble brilliance. Phil's faded suit of broadcloth, his frayed off-white shirt, his black shoe-string tie and greasy black sombrero in the cold light of day made him look what he really was: a broken-down tinhorn gambler — but now, in the ruddy light of the torch he looked almost regal. He stood erect like an actor in his greatest role, as the shouting of the mob, his audience, died to a murmur.

His rather reedy voice, made thicker and more resonant by liquor, rose above it all.

'These murderin' hellions've got to be taught a lesson. We've got to make an example of that greaser. If we don't this town of ours won't be fit to live in. Are we men or frightened mice?'

Cries of 'No! No!' came from the crowd. Frisco warmed to his own rhetoric.

'Are we goin' to let such border scum ride roughshod over us — burn our homes and slaughter our men?'

No! No! . . . Nobody saw the funny side of this last sentence of Frisco's. He had been in San Martini no more than six months and his home was a two-by-four bedsitter in a crummy lodging-house.

The orator became grandly savage.

'What we got to do is swing that greaser higher than a kite. Fly him so high that even his murderin' pards over the border will see him an' take warning. And if we can't get him out — if anybody tries to stop us gettin' him out . . . ' Phil paused dramatically his torch aloft, justice personified. His voice rang.

'We'll smoke out the whole damn

caboodle of 'em.'

A roar went up, torches waved wildly, and the whole mob of raging man-beasts swept down the street.

Frisco Phil stood grandly erect, his flaming brand held aloft, and watched as they swept past him. Then he tried to leap nonchalantly from the wagon.

He caught his heel in a trailing rope and sprawled headlong. Excruciating pain enveloped his right leg. He tried to rise but could not. The leg was broken. He bawled for help but nobody paid any attention. His brief spell of glory was over.

Like a wide sluggish stream splashing at the edges, tributaries running into it as doors opened and more people came out into the street, the blood-lusting mob swept on towards the jail. They did not need a leader now; they were all leaders, all one, like a savage monster with one black heart, one soul. The ruddy glow of the torches inflamed their faces, the open screeching mouths, the glaring eyes.

Their clamour now was like one single deep-throated roar.

Down at the jail the marshal and his deputy, the sheriff and the three Texas Rangers, heard it and waited. Their guns and rifles were ready. They were ready. Though an ill-assorted bunch they were all nerveless fighting-men. Not one of them had a thought of shirking such an issue as this. Men used to making their own decisions and fighting alone they could feel only contempt for mobs. Each one of them was confident he could handle such scum. Their minds would not allow them to think otherwise.

The mob poured down the street, slowed-down, and swelled out to a ballooning mass before the jail. The roaring subsided, then rose again to a clamour. It hummed, and above it all, single piercing voices called: 'We want the greaser!'

From the window of the sheriff's office a gun barked. The slug whined, far above the heads of the crowd, but it had the desired effect. They became silent.

It was Marshal Len Kane who spoke. His voice was authoritative. It carried menace too: he had handled mobs before.

'The greaser'll get what's comin' to him, make no mistake about that. But, as lawmen, we're opposed to lynchin' parties. There's quite a bunch of us here an' if you get too violent we aim to blast a load of lead right into the middle of you. I'd advise you all to go back to your drinkin', have a good night thataway. The greaser . . . '

Catcalls drowned his voice. After coming this far the crowd was not so easily turned aside — not even by Len Kane. In fact many of them felt secret pride at being able to buck this notorious man killer.

'Smoke 'em out!' yelled somebody. The torches waved uncertainly.

Inside the office the six men were a little uncertain too. To fire cold-bloodedly into that mass of people was not easy to do, even for the most callous of them. But do it they would if need be. They levelled their guns and waited. Len Kane was ready to give another spiel if he had the chance, but the clamour was intensified as the mob swayed back and forth, arguing among themselves. The front ranks were not so keen to attack now, but those behind kept pushing . . .

The attack, when it did come, came startlingly from another direction. Above the din of the mob, nobody heard the stealthy riders who approached the back of the town on their padded-hoofed horses, or hear the crash of the back door of the jail as it was burst open. The first inkling of this new development was when a rasping voice said: 'All right, gents. Freeze! You're well covered so don't turn around unless you want to commit suicide.'

The six lawmen did as they were told.

'Drop the guns,' said the voice. The

guns clattered to the boards.

'Now sheriff, turn an' throw me the keys to Pedro's cell.'

The sheriff turned, looking at the big man with the black kerchief round the lower half of his face. There were others with him, some of them still filing silently into the office. The sheriff unhooked the keys from his belt.

'Toss 'em,' said the big man.

He caught them expertly. It was then that Flash Kragar, half-hidden in the shadows, suddenly drew a derringer. Without a flicker of his eye, the big man fired. Kragar belched. The little gun clattered from his hand. He tottered out of the shadows. The lamplight shone on his lean, bloodless face, his yellow hair, a lock of it falling over his fading eyes. His mouth opened but no sound came from it. He pitched forward on his face. The cell-door clanged as one of the men let Pedro free. Stones clattered on the roof as the mob outside roared again, then somebody threw a torch.

The bandits began to file out of the

office. The big man was last. Before he went he said. 'Better stay where you are for a mite. I'll be watching this door an' as soon as it moves I'll start blastin'.'

The familiar voice again sent ripples up and down Jack Sharp's back. He winced. This sudden flamboyant, ruthless rescue of a comrade was typical of the man. The door banged.

The five men turned, reaching for their guns. The office was becoming filled with smoke as the roof caught fire. The mob was surging forward, but the lawmen were not concerned with them. The outer door banged. 'Come on,' said Marshal Kane and darted across the room.

He threw open the door and flung himself to one side. In the passage a gun boomed. The slug missed the marshal, but Gyp, who was behind him, gave a choking gasp and clutched at his chest. He crumpled to the boards.

Jack dropped on his knees and held the little ranger's head. As he looked into the wizened face, the man's eyes became blank. Jack let the head fall. There was murder in his eyes.

The outer door banged again. Jack beat the marshal to the cell-block and raced down the passage. The others, coughing now with the smoke, followed him.

The bandits had discarded the mufflers on their horses' hoofs, and could be heard thudding away across the mesa.

Jack ran to the stables. The lawmen's horses were still there.

'That's one mistake you made, Mert,' he said grimly.

★　★　★

Mert Scanlon, leader of the Gomez Boys, made another mistake that night, but that was after Fate took a hand in the game.

For the last few nights the San Martini mesa had been policed by stronger forces of night-riders. A bunch of these, composed of Horse V and

Pinwheel men, saw the flames shooting into the sky above San Martini and heard the approaching horsemen. They halted in a silent group. The bandits almost ran slapdash into them, but veered just in time. Firing was exchanged. Turning, the bandits tried to drive the night-riders back.

Then the four lawmen thundered up and added the music of their guns to the mêlée. Half-a-dozen bandits tumbled from their horses. One of them was Pedro Gabazo. Having just cheated a lynchmob's rope he died agonizingly with a bullet in his stomach.

The tall leader of the Gomez Boys barked a command and led his men in headlong flight. The posse, well-organized now gave chase, harrying their tails with redhot lead, demoralizing them.

Their sardonic triumph was snatched from their hands and turned on them with a vengeance. More of them bit the dust. Three of them, *vaqueros* in wide-brimmed sombreros, turned their horses. They held their hands above their heads to give themselves up. One of them was shot from the saddle by an over-eager cowboy. The other was hit on the head with a gun-butt and left in the grass to be picked up later.

The remaining bandits, a mere handful of them now, streaked for the border. They were still keeping their slender lead when they reached the Bridge spanning the Rio and clatterered over it.

They streaked for the hills, and there for a time the posse lost them.

It was Jack Sharp who pulled the last card from the bloody deck and turned it face upwards, thus sealing the doom of the Gomez Boys.

The familiarity of this particular stretch of the border hills set his brain working furiously. His mind harked back to one of the many scouting and hunting trips Mert Scanlon and he had made — and one in particular they had made in this very area. Maybe following unconsciously in his childhood footsteps, Mert had discovered the ruins of a large old house in the hills. The ruins of the fabulous Gomez fortress.

Did the son of Gomez remember that? Were his footsteps taking him there once more? Did he remember that his old pard, Jack, knew that secret valley too . . . Maybe he did.

'That's another mistake you made, Mert,' said Jack. Then he led the posse forward.

Once he had found the beginning of the trail his judgment was unerring and pretty soon they were approaching the silent ruins. They left their horses and on foot surrounded the stunted, craggy edifice. Then they advanced.

The skulking bandits were taken by surprise. Only three of them escaped annihilation in that fast, withering blast of lead. They made for the cellars. The tall leader was one of them, his mask off now, his pointed beard jutting from his handsome profile.

One of the three men fell before the

blazing two-guns of Marshal Len Kane, then the big man whirled, retaliating. Kane sagged at the knees, still firing. The big man went down, scrambled up again, and ran forward.

Marshal Kane lay still. Methodically like a firing-squad, the posse opened fire. Only Jack held his gun lax in his hand, and stood with hooded eyes.

Both the remaining bandits fell, but the big man managed to get to his knees. He crawled into the darkness of the cellar.

Despite shouts of 'Come back, you fool,' Jack went in after him.

He found him, dying like a rat in a corner. He dropped on his knees beside him.

'Mert,' he said huskily.

For a moment the dying man did not speak. His breath came in gasps. Then he said:

'You cain't . . . get me . . . outa *this* mess — pardner.'

'Take it easy, Mert,' said Jack. Remembering the countless times he

251

had said that before he was glad the shadows hid the pity in his eyes.

Mert said: 'I guess . . . I wuz allus a bad *hombre*. I — I . . . ' His head fell back.

Gently Jack lowered it to the ground. Mert beckoned feebly with his hand. Jack bent his head closer.

The words were a mere broken whisper.

'Look . . . after Judy — pard.'

'I will,' said Jack softly.

Mert could not hear him now but on the handsome face, serene in the shadows, was a little smile, as if he had known what the answer would be.

THE END

We do hope that you have enjoyed reading this large print book.

Did you know that all of our titles are available for purchase?

We publish a wide range of high quality large print books including:
**Romances, Mysteries, Classics
General Fiction
Non Fiction and Westerns**

Special interest titles available in large print are:
**The Little Oxford Dictionary
Music Book, Song Book
Hymn Book, Service Book**

Also available from us courtesy of Oxford University Press:
**Young Readers' Dictionary
(large print edition)
Young Readers' Thesaurus
(large print edition)**

For further information or a free brochure, please contact us at:
**Ulverscroft Large Print Books Ltd.,
The Green, Bradgate Road, Anstey,
Leicester, LE7 7FU, England.
Tel:** (00 44) **0116 236 4325**
Fax: (00 44) **0116 234 0205**

Other titles in the
Linford Western Library:

THE CHISELLER

Tex Larrigan

Soon the paddle steamer would be on its long journey down the Missouri River to St Louis. Now, all Saul Rhymer had to do was to play the last master stroke of the evening. He looked at the mounting pile of gold and dollar bills and again at the cards in his hand. Then, looking around the table, he produced the deed to the goldmine in Montana. 'Let's play poker!' But little did he know how that journey back to St Louis would change his life so drastically.

THE ARIZONA KID

Andrew McBride

When former hired gun Calvin Taylor took the job of sheriff of Oxford County, New Mexico, it was for one reason only — to catch, or kill, the notorious Arizona Kid, and pick up the fifteen hundred dollars reward the governor had secretly offered. Taylor found himself on the trail of the infamous gang known as the Regulators, hunting down a man who'd once been his friend. The pursuit became, in every sense, a journey of death.

BULLETS IN BUZZARDS CREEK

Bret Rey

The discovery of a dead saloon girl is only the beginning of Sheriff Jeff Gilpin's problems. Fortunately, his old friend 'Doc' Holliday arrives in Buzzards Creek just as Gilpin is faced by an outlaw gang. In a dramatic shoot-out the sheriff kills their leader and Holliday's reputation scares the hell out of the others. But it isn't long before the outlaws return, when they know Holliday is not around, and Gilpin is alone against six men . . .

THE YANKEE HANGMAN

Cole Rickard

Dan Tate was given a virtually impossible task: to save the murderer Jack Williams from the condemned cell. Williams, scum that he was, held a secret that was dear to the Confederate cause. But if saving Williams would test all Dan's ingenuity, then his further mission called for immense courage and daring. His life was truly on the line and if he didn't succeed, Horace Honeywell, the Yankee Hangman would have the last word!

MISSOURI PALACE

S. J. Rodgers

When ex-lawman Jim Williams accepts the post of security officer on the *Missouri Palace* riverboat, he finds himself embroiled in a power struggle between Captain J. D. Harris and Jake Farrell, the murderous boss of Willow Flats, who will stop at nothing to add the giant sidepaddler to his fleet. Williams knows that with no one to back him up in a straight fight with Farrell's hired killers, he must hit them first and hit them hard to get out alive.